For love and laughter with guido, woody, and sophia.

Measuring

Ann Tracy

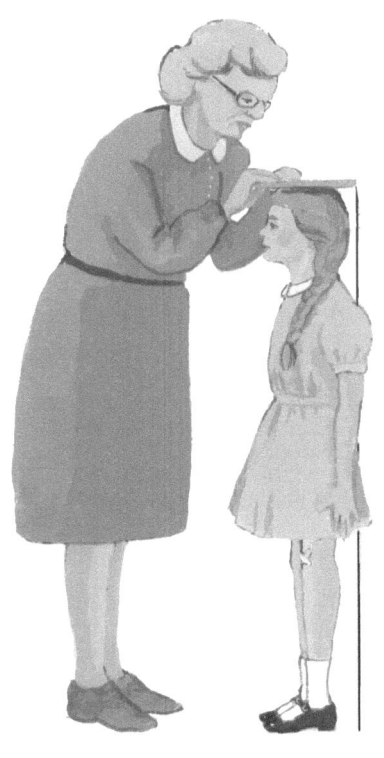

Spuyten Duyvil
New York City

ACKNOWLEDGMENTS

Thanks to Jenni Pickard for the computer skills that I have never possessed, and the knowledge of when to use them. Likewise thanks to the astute and skillful Ashley Bushmoore, unfailing friend. As for Virginia Cantarella, she and likewise her work have made me happy for many years. Blessings.   AT

Library of Congress Cataloging-in-Publication Data

Names: Tracy, Ann Blaisdell, author.
Title: Measuring / Ann Tracy.
Description: New York City : Spuyten Duyvil, [2020] |
Identifiers: LCCN 2020033963 | ISBN 9781952419065 (paperback)
Subjects: LCGFT: Short stories.
Classification: LCC PS3570.R26 M43 2020 | DDC 813/.54--dc23
LC record available at https://lccn.loc.gov/2020033963

Measuring

The summer my front teeth fell out I set myself to master long-distance spitting. What almanac lays out our psychic duties? Mine held that all right-minded children spit through their dental gaps, that never again would target spitting be such an accessible skill, that God meant me to exploit, not bury, this ephemeral talent. Crouched and puckering on the back steps, I'd aim at the rosebushes until my mouth ran dry. And miss, mostly. I wasn't good, only driven. But the Sunday morning when my friend Pearl MacKenzie and I balanced over the windowsill nearest the choir loft and spat between our hanging braids a prodigious distance onto the church woodpile, I knew, wiping my chin on my shoulder, the perfect joy of being in harmony with cosmic intent. Doing it right. Infant Platonism.

When you're a child you get used to being measured. Relatives back you up against calibrated door jambs, slide a cold pencil down the part of your hair to note on the paint whether you're as tall as your sibling or parent was at your age: *Alice, 8 yr 2 mo.* Teachers and nurses drop your IQ or your body into their scale pans on whim, and strangers' conversational overtures incline to assessment—what age, what grade, what acquaintance with decimals. Children are understood to be bored by this, but not offended. Anyhow, they're measuring each other, only the categories are more exciting—how far they can pee, or jump square-footed, number of incisors lost or collectibles acquired.

More important, to me, were my constant, secret measurements, not against my peers but against an ideal of style fed by pictures and stories. The snowmen we colored as a Friday afternoon treat always wore top hats; how could we feel right about our own snowmen, in a town with no top hats, about our bareheaded snowmen with features made from twigs and lopsided stones, not coal?

Juvenile fiction clouded the possible with visions of exotic accomplishment. Shouldn't I be building an ice boat, raising a monkey, solving crimes? Or flying kites, at least. Billy and Jane and Mary and Jack, those six-year-olds in the *Day by Day* reader who speak in one-syllable words, are making perfect, excruciatingly desirable kites at school. Mary's kite, in the picture, is bi-colored, pink on top and blue at the bottom. In the next chapter they all get those kites off the ground, too. How hard could it be? Worse, photographs of soapbox-derby cars filled me with such anxiety, such frustrated ambition—where could I ever find four unattached wheels?—that even now they call up little quivers of regret.

At the elbow of real life stood its ghostly, more glamorous double. I watched for the moment when they would merge, proving that life and art could be the same. Not that ordinary life was bad; not, for instance, that I didn't enjoy family picnics as they were, or found peanut butter sandwiches unacceptable fare. But so potent was the concept of PICNIC that I would have felt more justified than surprised if what I'd seen go into the cooler as Mallowpuff cookies came out as Victorian cup-custards with silver spoons. It could happen. Any day.

My parents seemed sometimes to be pursuing an analogous, though not identical, vision of what daily life should be. You could see it in their buying me the obligatory dog, a red cocker spaniel. I was seven. It was time for a dog. I had never thought of wanting a dog. We had been until then a purely cat-owning household, and none of us yearned for the dogs of our neighbors, but we'd been exposed to those calendar pictures of the kid in overalls going fishing with his best buddy the collie. Alas for art, the dog and I never became friends and confidants. In practice it proved disagreeably dim, drooly, rough-coated. Loutish and impenitent, it licked its shocking pink penis in front of company while the family cried, "You pull that right back in!" Bathing the dog made it smell worse, and none of us could teach it even simple tricks like begging. It persisted in standing up, I remember, between my father's supporting hands, while my mother pleaded, "*Knees*, Rusty, bend your *knees*!" This was typical, our allegiance to the notion of having a trick-doing dog in an environment where nobody knew how to train one.

But I had a second touchstone that kept home, however compromised, in perspective, and hope for its apotheosis alive: a hundred miles to the rural Maine north my dad's family farm defied measurement of any kind. To go to the farm was to go deeper into chaos, farther away from the colored scenes in my schoolbooks, from *The Weekly Reader* and Nancy Drew. There the thumb-slicked wooden container with which I scooped out chicken feed had been broken so long that the edges of the break were polished. The shed chamber, once no doubt furnished for hired men, seemed frozen in the aftermath of some bizarre disaster—1934 calendar on the floor, gray enamel chamber pot on its side in the corner, bird bones.

We went to the farm by driving east for a bit, then cutting north. Of the four roads leading out of town, the east soonest lost promise. South led to the cities, west at least to a larger town than ours—supermarket, eye doctor, hairdresser, jeweler. The east road at once left behind the mowed lawns and public buildings of the town center, dipped sharply, and headed for the woods.

Nan Royal's general store, at a crossroads ten miles on, was the first official sign of subsiding from the normal. Behind the fat white letters announcing Salada Tea, the windows were piled, heaped, with things not often wanted, and more hung from the ceiling. Grownups loved it that Nan could always find a lamp chimney or hay rake or peavey handle in the recesses of her hoard, but her popsicle selection, I felt, was poor. Quality of life changed visibly as we moved north, houses more often what we'd consider small; in their yards (less green than ours), painted tractor tires framed petunias or marigolds. Farther on, the house colors grew quirky—two walls blue, say, and two red, suggesting chance and makeshift. Artificial dwarves swarmed over the grass, plywood bears chased each other up real trees. Farther yet, tinier houses, portico-wide, totems made of auto parts in the dirt yards, clenched themselves against winter. We seldom saw any people, it seems to me now, only skinny dogs, the granite soldiers of Civil War monuments at occasional intersections, and little cemeteries cut back into the woods.

This was foreign territory—you could feel it. The skies were bigger, bleaker, the fields flatter than at home. Grass grew taller along the edges of the highway, up the middle of the logging roads and driveways. The bones of the past seemed to poke to the surface like the Precambrian shield through topsoil.

At about the time the woods stopped being interrupted by much of anything, my father would begin to sing melancholy car songs: "Danny Boy," about how the speaker may well be dead when his boy comes home, and a harrowing one about a lonely mother waiting in the old Maine homestead, and "Some day the silvery cord will break/ And I no more as now shall sing." He rarely sang except to offset dejection, which was particularly likely to get him on the long hauls to the farm. We watched for the marker of the only soldier who died in the Bloodless Aroostook War. Now and then a dirt road led off to the right or left, or we saw a solitary farm, often as not unpainted, in the midst of fields growing back to scrub. Things had evidently happened in this part of the world once, though, or who was lying in those cemeteries? One intersection of roads, where nothing but evergreens could be seen, my father remembered as having been called The Happy Corner. Happy why? Happy for whom?

Perhaps "happy" meant not much farther to go, my weary mother suggested.

"How much longer *do* we have to ride? I asked.

"Thirty-seven minutes," my father said with finality. He could do that anywhere in the hundred-mile trip and get it right.

At last, hot, bored, queasy, we turned a corner, drove up a hill, saw first the potato house and then the farm, and turned into the dirt driveway by the pump, scattering the hens. Nobody came out to meet us, but by the time we'd hauled our suitcases up the high step to the porch, Auntie Gyp had commanded her joints and stood up, Uncle Harris had caught on that something was happening, and they were glad to see us.

Uncle Harris and Auntie Gyp are my father's older brother and sister. As they cross the kitchen linoleum to greet us, both of them list perceptibly. Auntie leans on her cane, and Uncle Harris, getting up, does an odd, side-ways two-step of a stagger: now that I do it myself, I recognize it as the arthritic's dance to retain balance, but in Uncle Harris it somehow suggests that the planes of reality have tilted on him, that the uncooperative world is rolling under his feet like the deck of a ship.

They are not uncommon in my childhood, aunt-and-uncle pairs made of aging sisters and brothers, the residue of a family variously dissolved by deaths and marriages. My father decamped right after college, heading south to teach in our more seemly town. He has arthritis only in his hands, as though they were exposed (like Achilles' heel) before he could quite get the door shut behind him; and now those warped fingers, which won't lie orderly, side by side, hint at his origins even when he wears his best pin-striped suit.

After Auntie's death, not many months away now, Uncle Harris will live on twenty years, muddled, rumpled, unlucky, at the mercy of strange housekeepers. But it is Auntie whom I adore with my whole being. If there is nobody like her in the school readers, we might look for her in fairy tale: she is the anarchy in the core of my own heart.

Uncle Harris I neither loved nor hated. I gave him his share of that absentminded affection one gives to the harmless familiar, and might have given him more if I could have gotten a fix on who he was or what he wanted. His manner was friendly but not socially adept, his sudden pleasantries startling, unanswerable. "Oh ho, Casey Jones and the bantam rooster," he might, for instance, remark without warning, causing a conscientious grin to lock across my face.

In that pocket of the woods, men sometimes did say only the tag end of what they'd been thinking, but even in that terse context Uncle Harris's remarks were obscure, his mysterious mental processes the inward and spiritual counterparts of an outward and visible disorder. Uncle Harris wore a work shirt buttoned to the neck, a suit coat buttoned at the top, sturdy farm pants; why did they always look like someone else's clothes, totally random, and appear to be buttoned wrong when they weren't? His pockets bulged, his linings tore and hung down, his zippers jammed. He had driven his car through the back wall of the barn. He had been kicked by a dead cow with a posthumous muscle spasm. Only simple good will (his) and resolution (Auntie Gyp's) kept him from flying apart.

The aunt I knew may have been tempered a little for juvenile consumption, but I think not much, for when I would hear, years later, tales of her shrewd tongue and disregard of convention—how she had sent a gossipy minister packing, chased off with a shotgun a cousin who had left fleas on his previous visit (or, conversely, given away the best bed to a young couple who had none)—they failed to surprise. She carried around her like ether the whiff of perfect freedom.

For me it meant freedom to laugh at my elders; freedom to make mistakes like testing how tight I could hold a newly laid egg before it broke; freedom to wade, daydreaming, through waist-high grass for a whole breezy morning, or to lie on the carpet and memorize "The Song of the Shirt" with nobody asking me why, or to pull no-melody moans out of the parlor organ until a lesser aunt would have cracked. Lying in bed on her bad days, she taught me how to pitch pennies, mild gambling that made me feel freewheeling and joyfully wicked.

"Leave her be, she's happy," Auntie Gyp would order, and everyone would, as though happiness were reason enough.

She never commented on her own happiness or, likelier, her lack of it, but she sometimes sang me comic songs, that is songs like "The Last Rose of Summer" made comic by her hammy quavering. Lamentation for lost joy, as rendered by Auntie Gyp, implied that joy and sorrow were equally jokes. "Once I was happy, but look at me now— Out in the barnyard, a-milking the cow," she would carol, as if her transformation into an old cripple with felt slippers and shingled hair had been an Olympian party prank that only a spoilsport would fail to appreciate.

There had been another sister (not possible to imagine her as an aunt)—Lillian, who had died in childhood. Dad mentioned her now and then, "the Little Sister Who

Died." But she had been his big sister, not his little sister; "little" meant that he was old now and she was still a child. His phrasing caught the meaning of her. It was her death that mattered; Lillian revealed to me that children could die.

"How old *was* she?" I'd always ask, when she came up.

"Oh, about your age," my mother would say vaguely.

No matter how much older I got—six, seven, eight—I couldn't seem to outrun her. Every year I hoped to hear that she'd been younger than I, that I'd crossed some dangerous passage safely. But "Oh, about your age," my mother would say, and I'd be looking over my shoulder. I never asked my father. It seemed bad policy to refer to this potent, extraordinary loss. What if I shook his composure? At those ages I hated and feared emotion in adults.

In the summer of which I speak, we had gone up to the farm to help out between housekeepers. The neighbor girl who had been doing the heavy work and much of the cooking was getting married, while the old friend of Auntie Gyp's who had agreed to move in could not come before fall. Both my parents, I knew, were desperate to find someone for the interim and leave. Not that they minded the work. My father often came up to help Uncle Harris in the fields, and my mother, obsessive, would clean anything. But Mom had mistrusted the farm from giddyup, even though the whiskery neighbor who had burst into the kitchen on her first night there was only returning a butcher knife and not, as she had supposed, arriving to kill them. For her, the place stayed intractably alien. My father, conversely, must have felt ties that pained. By the summer of 1949 one could see early signs of the desolation that would overtake the house in earnest when all its women were gone: it was not dirty, but a little uncherished, unembellished, the company forks lying cold in newspaper, the vases unfilled. In the barn the stalls were empty: Boots and Fay, the workhorses with their lovely velvet noses big as plates, had died and not been replaced.

I myself took the farm's quirks for granted. I was still young enough to expect that every house except my own would smell foreign and follow peculiar customs. (The farm smelled of dust, chicken feed, hay, peonies, slop pails, damp, liniment, and molasses.) At my maternal grandmother's house they listened to "Pepper Young's Family" and ate puffed wheat for supper; Auntie Gyp and Uncle Harris kept the butter down cellar and dried their hands on a roller towel. Nothing told me that one set of domestic arrangements was more retrograde than the other. The parlor love seat with its hard, orange plush seemed an uncomfortable choice of furniture, less pleasant to sit on than our blue sofa at home, but that was none of my business. I could just as well lie on the floor to read *The Sinking of the Titanic and Other Great Sea Disasters*. The whole house had a bareness, a sparseness, a sense of some things worn down, like the nap on the organ pedals, and others put away in trunks.

I was drawn by the emptiness of the parlor (curiously called the "front," though the only parlor), which was not the shaded, formal room one sometimes still saw in the houses of the elderly, but open and sunny, dust motes dancing down in the light like pollen from the high weeds outside the window. The sofa, table, bookcase, organ, the lace curtains and the dim rug, were watched over by a large and massively framed photograph of my grandmother, circa 1900. And if I drew no other conclusions about norms, she must have seemed right to me, for I badly shocked Pearl MacKenzie, the first time I went to her house, by asking whether the lady framed large on their parlor wall was her grandmother.

"That's the *queen*," Pearl said, stunned by my ignorance. It was Victoria. Pearl's parents were Canadian.

By the second week at the farm we were running low on entertainment and my mother decided to clean out the closets in the back bedrooms. Auntie Gyp, consulted, didn't give a hoot as long as my mother was satisfied. She couldn't get upstairs anymore herself, so they must have seemed halfway like the closets in someone else's house.

These weren't ordinary closets, but mysterious eight-foot tunnels, one leading off to the left, the other straight in. I trailed along, hoping for discoveries. I had already played with the bureau drawers and found nothing more than a piece or two of underwear, some spilled powder and hairpins, and a booklet about the Dionne quints that I had carried off to my own bottom drawer in the kitchen's rolltop desk.

Down the hall Uncle Harris slept in the dark little room of his boyhood, in an iron bed that with a bureau and a linoleum made up all his furnishings. There he would lie at night and curse aloud, splendidly, at his aches, as though they had ears and intentions. Whole sentences would soar up from his rolling mumble: "You bejeezely godforsaken chaff-covered sons of bitches might let a man go to sleep!"

I giggled into my pillow, loving his inventiveness. Auntie slept downstairs on a cot now and kept her clothes in the back hall; the two good bedrooms were kept empty for company, for us, for hypothetical housekeepers.

We began with the closet in the best bedroom, which had the picture of two horses in a storm,the china washbowl decorated with flowers, and a tall bed painted brown and cream, with a medallion on the headboard. (What could the best bed have been like, I wondered, the one that Auntie had given away?) I drummed my heels on the side piece and watched my mother disappear into the closet, from which soon issued contented cleaning cries of "Whatever?" and "Honest to gosh!" and "Ugh!" Old overcoats and run-down shoes and a rotten parasol with deep ecru lace thumped out at intervals. I had some hope for the parasol, but the fabric shredded at my touch. After a bit my mother bailed out a flat black hat, faded purple pansies squashed on its crown. "I believe that's your great-grandmother Smith's Sunday bonnet!" she exclaimed, pleased. "Your dad's told me how she used to sail into church with it, looking proud as royalty."

"In *this*?" I said, turning it incredulously.

"It would have looked pretty when it was new," she told me. "Most things do."

This was a notion I hadn't considered.

"Even old-fashioned dresses all rotted out under the arms?"

She struck a pose. "Ma's dark green delaine with little leaves like strawberries," she quoted. We were all big quoters at my house.

"*Little House in the Big Woods,*" I countered. "Oh." I hat-

18

ed like poison to admit that something I didn't already know could be true, but this new insight into the effects of time attracted me. I teetered on the edge of acceptance.

Then, with a pertinence she could never have staged, my mother said, "See what's in these, will you," and dropped three stockinet shoe bags on the quilt.

I opened the smallest first, and there—clean, un-creased, not even scuffed on the soles—lay a pair of high-topped button boots for a girl a little smaller than I. It was like time travel. I could see how good they would have looked on the shelf in the store, pale green canvas with shiny brown leather toes, buttons dark as blackberries, and I hungered to be buying, owning, wearing them.

"Look!" I croaked.

"Daddy had a little sister who died, you know," she said, as though I didn't know Lillian like my own shad-ow. "The poor little girl must have died before she got to wear them." The sentimental tremble in her voice made me cross and itchy.

"So she was younger than me," I said accusingly, to head her off.

"Maybe just smaller," she murmured, squelching once again my hope of outfooting death. "I suppose we shouldn't throw them out, but what they're good for I don't know."

"They were hers," I said, but I meant more. They were a window.

"Oh dear, you'll be a pack rat like your father," said my mother, recovered. "I suppose there's no help for it."

I hated to let go of those shoes, but I hated worse to expose some tender, private part of my mind by showing how they mattered. I set them back on the bed and leaned my forehead with affected boredom against the windowpane.

"Hey," I said, "there's a car coming." Gravel crunched. "I think it's Estelle and Bern."

"Oh Lord," my mother said. "That means extra for supper. Come on. We can finish up here tomorrow."

"Better sit up, Harris; Bern and Stelle are coming," my mother warned as we passed the kitchen couch on our way to the yard, where the sisters were getting out of their high car with a mannerly slowness that would let us catch up and encourage them.

"*Oh* God," said Uncle Harris, levering himself upright with an agitated rattle of his false teeth.

Bern and Estelle, old family friends, were both private-duty nurses in the nearest big town, and each was in her own way formidable. Bern, shorter and more muscular, wore her hair pulled back in a fierce bun. She dearly loved a fight. She had got all the pepper in the family gene pool, and judging by Estelle's blandness, most of the salt as well. Estelle was thick-ankled, deliberate, tenacious. Her slow voice cracked in the middle of her sentences. Uncle Harris didn't object to Bern, her battle reports tickled him, but Estelle made him nervous, for she was, amazingly but unmistakably, courting him. She had been doing this more or less forever. They were both in their late sixties, though Uncle Harris looked older. He made no acknowledgment of her advances. "Bern and them," he'd say, denial in full flower, "Bern and them brung me a cake."

"I picked some wild strawberries, Harris," said Estelle,

setting a kettle down on the table. My mother made admiring noises over it.

"Gyp likes 'em, I guess," said Uncle Harris in a high, desperate voice, running his hands through the hair at his temples, standing it on end.

"I guess Harris likes them too," Estelle said with a touch of coyness that sat oddly on her tall, loose frame. "Don't you remember the berries we found, Harris, when we went fishing up Monument Stream?" This was crafty. Monument Stream was Uncle Harris's Shangri-La.

"Up Monument, up Monument, that's the place to catch 'em!" he said, making a gallant dash at conversation.

"We should do it again sometime," she said. "Come on out and sit on the glider and talk to me. You work too hard running this farm, Harris."

"Running this farm," Auntie Gyp said to me *sotto voce*. "Your father and I run this farm, I guess. Your Uncle Harris couldn't run a two-hole backhouse!"

That killed me, the boldness of the image, the slight rudeness of "backhouse" instead of my mother's "johnny house," the absurdity and confidentially of it. I squealed with delight, my hand over my mouth. "Heee!" I exploded through my fingers, "Hee!"

"That child has found a tee-hee's nest," said my mother. "What ails her?"

"Got the galloping he-cups," said my aunt, winking. "Go on in the pantry, you plaguey brat, and eat some sugar for it."

Understanding that Auntie meant to slide me an extra treat, I poured a teacup half full of sugar and sat on the counter to lick it out while I listened with some interest to Bern's vigorous account of browbeating the police. I knew that later, blithe and treacherous, we would laugh at her language—she said "audience" for "ordinance," "wagger" for "wager"—but I would have preferred to hear the glider conversation, for just what Estelle wanted, and why, was a bafflement. I thought her boring, able to talk only about berries and fish and nursing, and those not interestingly, but nonethe less the advantage seemed to be all on her side.

But it was not by the conversation on the porch that Estelle had made progress after all, for where insinuation and flirtation had failed, a bold gesture succeeded. She had made my parents and Auntie Gyp an irresistible offer: she would come and keep house for the rest of the summer. Dad broke it to Uncle Harris at supper, to which Bern and Estelle had after all not stayed.

"Well, Harris," he said, playful in his relief, "looks like we've found you a willing housekeeper."

We watched comprehension dawn. Do bright siblings take these small revenges on slow ones all their lives?

Uncle Harris started up in his chair. "I wish I had a little barn about a mile from hell!" he cried, and fell back.

"Now Harris," teased Auntie Gyp, "you know you like 'Stelle's biscuits."

"Them biscuits ain't bad," he agreed, comforted.

When Auntie was lying down that evening, I crept in and sat on the edge of her cot. She shifted to make room for me. "Auntie," I whispered, "excuse me for asking, but *why* does 'Stelle want Uncle Harris?"

Auntie whooped and sat up. "Go fetch the album from the parlor," she ordered when she could speak, "and bring that lamp closer."

I tugged in ten pounds of red velvet and nickel hasp and dropped it on the bed.

"Now who's that?" she asked, opening the pages to a young man with a crooked necktie. I studied the handsome face, the cowlick, the dimple in the chin. It didn't look like anyone I knew. I shook my head.

"That's who 'Stelle thinks she's chasing," she said. "That's Harris forty years ago. She doesn't see the old man you do."

I cast about for something to say, worthy to meet this thunderclap but covering, a little, my amazement. "Mom says most things look pretty when they're new," I heard myself offer weakly.

"Does she?" said Auntie Gyp. "Well it's the damned truth. I wasn't bad myself once, can you believe that?"

"And was Estelle pretty too?"

"Nope," said Auntie. "'Stelle was always plain as bread and twice as good."

"Uncle Harris likes bread," I joked.

"He doesn't like 'Stelle," said Auntie Gyp. "My Lord, I think he even likes that old battle axe Bern better than her. It's pitiful, but there we are."

Indeed we were. Who could have guessed that those grizzled adults looked at one another and saw someone else, someone who drove them to frenzies of berry picking and courtship? Someone from the world before I was there to measure it, that other, contiguous world where Lillian left her shoes.

When we finished the closets the next day and dug up half an ancient, fly-specked Sears Roebuck catalogue, I fell upon it and claimed it. I had gotten hooked on the past.

"You don't want that filthy book," my mother scolded. She meant germy, not obscene. She worried about germs year round, but especially in the summer, polio season, when it seemed that a bogey who struck at beaches and parades might lurk anywhere, pop out of closets or public cups to maim me. Merely by suggesting that my neck hurt I could drive her into such a frenzy (phoning pediatricians, invoking the names of local crippled children) that I rarely said so even when it was true.

"It's not very dirty; I just want to see it," I argued, and headed for the porch glider. Downstairs it would be harder for her to act as though Auntie's closet was a contagious ward in Rangoon.

I found in the catalogue, to my delight, quite a few familiar objects—close equivalents of the stereoscope, the stove, the furniture in my bedroom. The parlor lamp and the dish patterns looked familiar. Dad's family had evidently owned the right things.

When I came to the organ/piano section I stopped. Here was a good deal of hoopla, twenty-five-year Bonds of Indemnity, arguments and inducements for buying an instrument. The Imperial Grand Organ, not unlike the one in the parlor, cost as much as a whole dining-room set. Was ours as good as that? I tiptoed into the parlor through the seldom-used front door and looked it over. Faded red fabric behind fancy cutouts in the wood; two rows of stops to pull, smooth and black as licorice; carpeted pedals; music rack and swiveling lamp stands. It appeared to be a good one.

I lay over the stool on my stomach, rotating and thinking. Why had my relatives bought this thing? It, too, was new once; it must have been bought and brought in at some sacrifice. I had never seen any of them play it, though judging by the worn pedals, someone had done so at one time. Had my grandmother played? I tried to imagine what *they* must have imagined, choosing it, perhaps an attractive family group around the parlor organ having a sing-song. In what world could the reality have happened—my grandmother alive and pumping, Harris with his clothes all awry, my wiseass aunt, doomed Lillian, the brainy little boy who would turn into my father? As far as I knew, nobody in my family could carry a tune for long. And what had they sung, "Once I was Happy"? What impossible, misguided vision of domestic rightness had they been pursuing?

I stood up. God help us, it wasn't just me, dreaming in my improvable world. In all their loss and chaos, they'd been measuring too.

Boundries

Take a dip, wet a line—our language reflected our caution. The family credo held that we liked the lake best on the rare days when it was flat as a mirror, when the water, smooth and dense as silver on our skins, made cool bracelets at the line where it met the air. There was a bigger lake than ours, Grand Lake itself, but we never ventured beyond its mouth. Despite our life jackets, despite the sponsons on our motor boat that would save us from capsizing, we only hovered at the big lake's edge, giddy with admiration, then turned our prow and headed back to camp. Too much water. But secretly, perversely, I fancied a good blow, the boat jumping and slapping as we ran for harbor. When I have dreams nowadays of our camp, our cottage on the Canadian shore of East Grand Lake, thirty-foot waves sweep in through the porch screens until we're washed from our chairs to swim like minnows in a bait trap.

Any possible implications of sponsons notwithstanding, in those early summers I was led to believe that Nature meant us well. Didn't the mothering woods give us raspberries, spruce gum, hazelnuts, a gold root that healed canker sores, jewel weed to hang on our ears? The brightness in the bellies of fish pleased me too—-my father cleaned them in a rocky spot where shore met forest. Only when Cousin Glaydee ripped the guts through the mouth of a still living fish did we catch a clear flash of human predation and turn away. Too much truth.

Crossing the border into Canada and heading for camp, we believed ourselves to be entering a world of relaxed standards, We could see it in the Customs Buildings themselves, the US building in brick, squared on its concrete base, the green clapboard Canadian building beside the wild roses at the edge of the lake. The Americans seemed to suspect our intentions, while the sole Canadian officer, who had sometimes left a note and gone home for lunch, was too polite to give the trunk of our car more than a cursory glance. We imagined that Canadians didn't care much about laws, a happy-go-lucky people, and we thrilled with vicarious outlawry when the local MP jacked deer and dragged the carcasses over our sea wall: Canada, sweet land of liberty.

Thus at camp we cast aside aside the tasteful restraint of our winter lives and wallowed in license—Fiestaware on the oilcloth; apple-green chairs trimmed in Chinese red. Though I would never have marked the glossy pages of my library at home, at camp I was allowed to improve with watercolors the illustrations on my story books' rough paper. Herbie, Derbie and Kerbie, going to the zoo, balanced red, blue, and orange heads on their stick necks. We did not paint our own bodies except by accident, but we might have. We wore older, rattier, more comfortable and sometimes fewer clothes than at home; in the boat we sang with tuneless abandon; we wasted our evenings in Cribbage or Rummy or Hearts. When my father went out to buy a newspaper he quite often brought back a handful of candy bars for no reason but the indulgence of it: we were at the lake.

He bought those candy bars at the hermaphrodite's store, a low red shed with a Lucky Strike sign nailed to the short end. Among ourselves we spoke of the proprietor in respectful tones, as of some incarnate mystery, the man-woman, one more escape from winter's rules. That frail gray person in a man's suit and a well-of-loneliness haircut stood behind the counter and refused to be classified. You could look look into those eyes until you staggered, and go back to the sharp-edged world empty handed.

"Madam," my father would ask, undone by courtliness and the need for definition, "would you have any six-penny nails?" Or perhaps in another summer, "What do I owe you, Sir?" In my teens I would cringe at this troubling of shadows, sure as soon as I heard either salutation that the other was less offensive.

Though not up to the hermaphrodite's standard of interest, other persons cut loose from custom or domesticity peopled our summer lives. At home, adults rarely dined in one another's homes, only children stayed for supper. At camp, my parents' friends the Burtons might come for a week at a time with their children, their boy Neddy crossing family lines to become my brother. Or later my friend Pearl would stay at camp with us for whole nights and days, a mammoth sleepover. More permanent fixtures of that summer world were my father's two cousins, Osgood and Glaydee. Osgood (from grandmother's side) was a lifelong bachelor, while I had heard my mother say that Glaydee (from grandfather's side), a generation older, had once incredibly had a wife and son. Now both cousins seemed equally sexless, dried out, juiceless as strip fish, though their styles were very different. Consider these scenes:

One: Osgood is watching Neddy Burton and me. Our parents have gone out to fish after supper, and we're considered too young to take, though too old to put to bed like babies. He is reading aloud to us from *The Saturday Evening Post,* a Will Cuppy essay about the habits of wombats. We stand beside him in our overalls, four or maybe five, laughing at the parts we're sure are funny. Osgood is wearing a remarkably grubby pair of white flannels from the Twenties. He's the only grownup we've ever seen in white pants. An ascetic, scholarly man with an ironic wit, Osgood is courteous to children though not effusive, and can be expected not to scold or criticize us. We feel safe with him. Rising to his style of care puts a little strain on us, though.

Osgood's camp, across the lawns from ours, smells of print and paper. Besides his glass-fronted bookcase, he has stacks of magazines two feet high, *Post* or *Colliers* mostly, with the occasional *Life.* His walls are only bare studding turned dark, not as nice as our knotty pine, but objects hung on the studs are significant. World War One army helmet, college diploma with his name in Latin. He lives hedged and protected by words.

Two: Glaydee, who lives at our camp from spring thaw to fall freeze, has been persuaded to show Neddy and me his most precious object. He is grudging, for he resents all visitors, especially children. He thinks it's his camp. He tolerates me and sometimes calls me an imp, which my amused parents say is as close to a term of affection as Glaydee gets. Gaunt and brooding, he opens his knife and cuts a square of tobacco. Brown spit stains the lines around his mouth. We watch his slow hands fold up the knife, reach for the tackle box. The cuffs of his navy cardigan are ragged.

His only attraction for us is the totem in the box. We breathe more quickly while he extracts from dirty hooks and lines a plain wooden egg about two inches long, dark with the juices of fishing. He pulls it in half. The egg inside is fancier, printed with green swoops that could be a plant, could be a snake, but it's gone now, and the third egg rolls in his hand, looking older than the others, its narrow stripes pale and primitive. We lean over it. Inside on a wad of cotton batting lies a naked woman, shocking in her stark china whiteness. Her hair is inky black, her lips red. Glaydee waxes reverent. "That's my little lady," he says, as he always does. "I never go fishing without her." His tone adds to the weight of seeing her. Could she possibly be magical? This fishy old man seems to think so.

I never thought to ask why Glaydee lived at our camp. He was there by some act of charity that I took for granted, skulking along the shore when he wasn't out in his flat-bottomed boat dealing death. In winter he lived with other kinfolk, and although he spoke little he would sometimes tell me about the children of that house, Joanne and Bobby, and how much they loved him. How Joanne especially would jump onto his lap and call him "my Glaydee." This seemed so tall a tale that any implicit reproach missed me. Could anyone be drawn to Glaydee's dour face, his dark old clothes that reeked of tobacco? I was too young to wonder what, if he was lying, his fantasies might mean.

Glaydee hated Osgood with a depth of bitterness unaccustomed in our family. He refused to speak his name. "That feller," he called him. "That feller stole my motor." This unlikely accusation had been the start of the trouble, as far as my parents could tell. Now when Glaydee mowed our lawn he stopped with vicious precision at the property's edge, leaving Osgood's lawn a narrow strip of field—daisies, alfalfa, devil's paintbrush. Osgood would put out his lawn chair and recline among his weeds, reading with provocative calm while Glaydee raged speechlessly over the rocks. Though irritating Glaydee must have seemed a bonus, Osgood's lack of response to the unmown grass was genuine. He went his own detached way, as free from definition as the hermaphrodite but happier.

We sometimes saw Osgood in the winter. He and my father, heads of different schools, met on business, perhaps made a social call if one was in the other's town. Away from his white flannels and magazines, wearing a tie, Osgood seemed somewhat removed, like a friend glimpsed through window glass, but he fit as neatly into the habits of our contained winter world as into the letting down of summer. Glaydee was impossible to imagine in our winter setting; all the things that gave him character were at the lake. I occasionally dragged home from camp a burlap bag of colored stones, pieces that had caught my attention for their shapes, textures, veins of quartz, resemblance to other objects. At home, like scraps of birch bark or dried tree fungus, they seemed sad bits of debris. I would have expected Glaydee outside his context to lose meaning in the same way.

Nonetheless and against all likelihood, he came for a visit the winter I was eight. His regular hosts were ill, perhaps, or expecting more important guests—I don't know now, nor do I know how long he stayed, though I presume that my visceral response, all winter, is wrong. Suddenly there he was, a little better clothed, less surly and territorial, but himself a displaced object from camp, as unsuitable in the living room as a calendar picture of The Old Judge. We housed and fed him and left him to his own devices, as was our summer custom.

One day he called me to the sofa, where he was looking at *The Ladies' Home Journal*. How could I not have fled at the sight of that anomaly, as startling as a buzzard knitting lace? Could this be Glaydee, saying "Come help me look at these pictures"? What kind of help could a person need, I wondered. He never looked at pictures with me at camp. Was this for him, as camp was for us, the other place, the place where habits changed? I perched on the edge of the cushion.

He moved till our thighs touched, then spread the open pages over both our laps, but more over mine. He reached across my shoulders and gave me a little hug, as though he were another sort of adult entirely. "How's that?" he asked.

"Fine," I said, amazed but guarded.

While Glaydee turned the pages, we made stilted conversation. "That cake looks good, don't it?" "Yes, Glaydee, it does."

His left hand slid from the pages and ferreted under my skirt. His fingers, knotted with arthritis like my father's but with longer nails, trailed across the skin near the edge of my underpants and slid beneath the elastic. I gazed hard at the magazine, pondering the duty of a hostess in the face of such peculiar rudeness. *This is a Watchbird watching a coward. This is a Watchbird watching you!* Rattling on about the illustrations, I raced through the pages of the *Journal*, closed it, shot to my feet. Over, the lunacy was over.

But of course it wasn't, of course we hadn't looked at those pictures in enough detail, hadn't even started on *McCall's, Life,* the other lap-sized magazines. Of course from time to time Glaydee caught me alone in the living room. We looked at ads, we looked at illustrations, we looked at photographs, distractions to cover the assault of his ancient, trembling fingers. What could one do? He was part of camp, the place we all adored, not a very attractive part but as far as I knew not an optional one. Might not the whole fabric unravel if he was torn out of it? He was Glaydee.

Or was he? One day the magazine opened to a picture of a bride and groom in a hail of confetti. "They don't have as much fun as we do, do they?" he said, his voice unsteady, and I thought, "You damned old fool," tasting the release of it. Who would have guessed that inside the redoubtable Glaydee lay not some shocking surprise, hard as china, but a slough of tedious folly nowhere near so attractive as the polychrome guts of fishes? His fingers were an embarrassment, but his silliness blew obligation away. Not long after his visit ended I told my mother, who told my father.

I never saw Glaydee again, nor did we speak of him. At the lake, Osgood soon took dinner with us every day; no need for both of them to heat up a stove, said my mother. Camp life closed seamlessly over Glaydee's absence. I had been wrong. One day, finding his tackle box under the stairs, I requested the wooden egg, and with it I bore away the naked china woman and whatever luck she might possess.

Glaydee's bed being empty, we were sometimes, soon nearly always, accompanied to camp by old Ted, who did odd jobs for us at home. "Ted loves to come to camp, I couldn't leave him behind," my father would say helplessly when my mother would inquire *why*, in the name of *heaven*, just *once* the family couldn't get a way without old *Ted*.

Ted's style was as different from Glaydee's as Osgood's was. Where Glaydee had been grim, Ted was mindlessly cheerful. Where Glaydee had been reclusive, Ted was expansive. Where Glaydee had been taciturn, Ted wouldn't shut up. Ted was tall and barge-footed and goofy. He had a relentless memory for songs about kissing widows and old maids, and for narrative poems of many verses, but no memory at all for designated chores. He ate all the fruit in the bowl, he bid sky-high with only low cards in his hand, he tangled his fishing line into a mass that filled the bottom of the boat, and once he forget his belt and lost his pants on the streets of Houlton.

His willingness made it necessary to forgive him. Out on the lake my father passed him the anchor rope.

"Tie it around the seat, Ted," he said.

"Oh, around my feet?" said Ted, starting to loop it around his ankles. There it was. He was an idiot but he was ready to tie the anchor around his feet when my father (as he supposed) asked him to. His buffoonery colored a jollier if more exasperating period of camp life than the one Glaydee had stalked through.

Ted not only sang about kissing widows and old maids, he fell in love with them. He would give eccentric gifts (thimbles, satin aprons) to the objects of his passion, thinking himself engaged thereby, weeping with desolation when he found it wasn't true. The adults in my life thought this a high old joke but could never head him off at the start, his attachments were that unpredictable. They paid no attention when he began to spend time at the hermaphrodite's store, to which he furtively hiked, not asking for rides. He would bring back small items to my mother to explain his having gone.

"I thought you could use this fly paper," he'd say.

"Well," my mother would say, baffled. "Thank you."

His songs and recitations grew so soppy that adults sometimes fled the room. He lost his fishing pole overboard, he upset his dinner plate on his lap. My friend Pearl and I relished the chaos and egged on his performances just to watch the grownups scatter.

One evening as the sky was darkening he broke silence. "Two hearts," he said dreamily.

"We're playing Rummy, Ted" my father said.

"She's a good girl," said Ted.

"All right," said my father.

"Her at the store," Ted said, turning redder. "She's a good girl." His voice trembled with emotion.

Pearl and I at the other end of the table froze over our comics, fascinated. Even for Ted, "girl" seemed a glib assumption. In the trembling of his voice I heard echoes of Glaydee and was thankful not to be the one Ted was fancying.

"I could take her out to Houlton to the picture show," he went on, "but first I'd like to get her out of that suit." Then he must have heard himself, or seen signs of strangled mirth in my parents, because he blushed yet more deeply, guffawed, dropped his cards, and began to hum. Pleased, we abandoned our reading for what we had reason to hope would be a better show.

"Oh when I was single I knew what to do," he sang archly.

The adults looked startled. "You two go to bed this minute!" my father cried, sounding cross.

The injustice of it! We stormed up the stairs and lay down with our ears on the floor, but the informative lyrics had been suppressed.

"Do you suppose Ted *ever* knew what to do?" Pearl whispered. We giggled until our lips made breathy blotches on the linoleum.

"I guess if Ted could get that suit off he might find a surprise," my father said the next day. He didn't say it to Pearl and me, that would have been improper, but he said it to Osgood and my mother, with us in the room, and we understood it to be a kind of apology.

Osgood said he guessed if that poor creature could see inside Ted's head the surprise would be mutual.

"What do you suppose the inside of Ted's head would look like?" my father mused.

"Mother Hubbard's cupboard," suggested Osgood.

"Might find some old sheet music and a dime novel," my mother said.

They assumed that Ted was susceptible to passion because he was empty-headed to start with, but I thought I knew better. It was the other way around. Because what about Glaydee? Was Ted's certainty that the storekeeper was a girl any dimmer than Glaydee's conviction that we were both having fun? It was passion itself that skewed a person's sense of boundaries, and desire was a boat without sponsons, its anchor looped around the helmsman's feet.

In the Year That King Uzziah Died

My father expected disaster. Not ordinary things gone awry, flat tires and chimney fires. He would have assumed that most ordinary things could be managed into going right. What he foresaw was cataclysm, national or global events that could make "ordinary" lose its meaning. War on American soil. Economic collapse. Things, perhaps, beyond his naming. Coming out of deep thought he would tell us suddenly, unsolicited, his plan to get a horse and wagon, if war was declared, and drive us to live on the farm. No, I imagined, not to live: to hide from the enemy and subsist like rats in a cornpile. I could see too clearly the slow, rattling journey north, explosives falling around us.

Or picture my brother Murphy, still too young to talk, who has finished his breakfast and stands beside our father's place with his mouth open, cadging bites. "If there's another depression you won't be having two hen's eggs for breakfast," my father warns this tiny figure in Doctor Dentons, morning after morning, as he spoons most of his own egg into the waiting mouth.

Our apocalyptic expectations were encouraged by the church as well, Baptists like other fundamentalists being drawn with irresistible fascination to the last book of the Bible. It's inevitable, given the assumption that the Bible is a kind of supernatural *Wall Street Journal*. There, revealed not very plainly to St. John the Divine, was the authorized prediction of our likely end. Every few years some new minister, fresh-faced, wild-eyed, would erect a nine-foot flannelgraph chronology of the Last Days, and settle down to preach about it.

Woe to pregnant women then, he would say happily, *and woe to the mothers of infants and small children when they flee to the hills that provide us no real protection! Woe to the remnant left behind after the saved are caught up to Heaven: for any chance at Salvation they must see through the propaganda and reject the Mark of the Beast, though without it they can never buy and sell or stay alive. Ah, but worse than woe to those who take the Beast's mark on their bodies.* Too clear that the Truly Saved would look forward to all this carnage: if we dreaded it, chances were we'd be around for it.

What with one thing and another, Gloria Hall's announcement that her grandfather was a prophet fell on fertile ground.

That it should be Gloria whose grandfather prophesied was both surprising and not. On the side of surprising, she and her family were only occasional churchgoers, quite as likely to choose the alternative entertainment of the stock-car races, though we supposed they believed something like we did, but perhaps with less hymn singing. On the other hand, there was a joyful unpredictability about the Halls that might produce a prophet or a human cannonball as soon as a grocer. Gloria's household included an aunt and uncle in her own age range, which I thought exotic, and remarkably non-judgmental parents. "Jerry threw the axe at Kate, it stuck right in the shed door," she might announce as she took off her snowsuit in the cloakroom, grinning at the excesses of her kin, but she never mentioned any punishments even after, as sometimes happened, she got through a dull hour by taking her clothes apart. Once she unraveled the whole of a new orange sweater, giggling softly to herself through the day as she pulled and wound up the yarn, the sweater growing shorter on her body. She was neither mischievous nor unhinged, only pure-heartedly amused at what happened when she pulled the yarn end. Impossible not to like her.

She and Pearl and I were mooning about on the swings. We were at the age when swing habits diverged. Bold contemporaries like to pump, standing up, until the swing arced backwards over the frame, scribing a circle in the air. Teachers tried, in vain, to discourage this, for first graders standing too close would have their heads laid open by the swing seat and grope back to their classrooms sheeted in blood. Gloria and Pearl and I liked to swing slowly, thoughtfully, like old ladies on a porch glider, growing dreamy and confiding. On this warm and buzzing day near the end of Spring 1951 the hard-core swingers had turned to dodgeball and we had the swings to ourselves. We pushed with one foot at a time, our heels drifting over the dust. Pearl was sucking on one of her pigtails and humming "Cruisin' Down the River." It came through her hair like a tune on a wax-papered comb, but fluffier.

"Guess what," Gloria said, "Gram and Gramp Hall are coming to live with us. Ma's mad and so is Jerry. Jerry's awful mad—they're getting his room, and he has to go sleep with Tommy, and Tommy still pees the bed sometimes. Gram crochets afghans all day but she'll only do orange. Gramp's a prophet."

She said it so easily—Tommy pees, Gram crochets, Gramp prophesies.

Pearl and I woke up in a hurry.

"A real prophet?" I asked, pleased.

Pearl spit out her braid, hoping for she-bears.

"I guess he's real; he says he is," said Gloria. "He told me one time how God said he should get the car out of the barn because he'd need it. So now he says God tells him things and he's a prophet."

"What else?" I asked.

"Well," Gloria said, angling her swing closer, "he says the world is going to end in 1953."

With round eyes Pearl and I stared at Gloria, at each other, at the doomed landscape. Gloria had handed us a yarn-end that would unravel the known world. We couldn't resist it. What were trees and skies and recess and Hershey bars compared to the power of this wild, private revelation? We gave them all up and believed at once, hugging the knowledge to our pre-pubescent chests. Anyhow, 1953 was ages away,

"Are we telling anyone else?" I asked.

"Elaine?" Pearl suggested. "Because she's so religious?"

Elaine was a thin, pale child with a gift for extemporaneous prayer, a form of torment in vogue at our church. Requested to pray aloud at Christian Endeavor, she would rise with a little sigh and address the Lord seriously and deferentially; she could think of things to pray for, missions in foreign fields, for instance, while most of us on that religious hot spot could think only of throwing up.

"Okay," said Gloria, "but just her. Just us four."

Elaine, as expected, was both pleased and interested.

She was, of all of us, most loosely attached to the sublunary world and most bent on heaven. In 19th-century Sunday-school tracts she would have been dead already.

"Nineteen fifty-three," she said with reverential cheer. "Well. Where in the Bible did he say he found it?"

"Didn't say," said Gloria. "Just said Bible." Elaine sometimes made us terse.

"Gotta be Revelations," Pearl said. We all used the plural when we spoke of that book.

"Let us meet," said Elaine, "to study it for ourselves."

And so we became a club. This was good, girls did it in books.

We met in rotation at one another's houses, reckoning that by the time our parents noticed a pattern we'd all be near to dead. At Gloria's there was always a good chance the prophet himself would show up and add a piece to the puzzle. "In the year that King Uzziah died, the Lord laid a coal upon my lips!" he might exclaim, wandering, wrapped in an orange afghan like a proto-Krishna. "Do you understand, children?" Not altogether, but we liked it.

"When the Trumpet of the Lord shall sound and time shall be no more/ And the morning breaks eternal, bright and fair—" We sang that hymn with ephemeral October, bright and fair, glowing outside the church windows, and sweat slightly at our hairlines and on the palms of our hands. We were the only ones left who knew how soon that trumpet would sound, and we were dug a year and a half deeper into the world than we'd been on that spring day when Gloria let us in. We didn't want to leave after all.

In November I found a loophole. "Aren't we supposed to have the Second Coming before the end?" I asked Elaine doubtfully. She listened to sermons harder than I did.

"I believe you're right," she said, relieved. "And there'd be a broadcast if it happened, wouldn't there?"

But there was not— only, in the the family's kindling box, a cloud-formation newspaper photo that looked like Jesus. Only parents casually kissing us goodnight, and the dawning of 1953. That spring we asked our mothers to teach us lazy-daisy and French knots: it appeared that we would be embroidering pillow cases for our hope chests after all.

The Fever
of the Bone

My generation fell in love with its own bones: the shoe-store x-rays (devised just in time for us and found just after us to be lethal) showed at the press of a button not only how our feet fit into the outlines of our shoes, but an amazing bonus—how our bones fit into the outline of our feet. We couldn't get enough of watching our foot bones dance when we wiggled our toes; we'd be waiting for new-shoe season like we waited for Halloween, and for similar reasons. Older, even, though we acted casual, we couldn't resist slipping our feet into the slots for a fast caper of the luminous greens. But most of all on the jittery edge of adolescence, twelve, thirteen, the uncanny x-ray light elucidated for us one mystery of the flesh, at least: there really was, as rumored, a skeleton under our skin.

News about either flesh or death seemed hard to come by in those days when we not only lurched between states of our own lives but staggered a bit as the national consciousness shifted. Along with our childhoods the familiar Forties had passed away and the Fifties had arrived with a new agenda, bleaching this, burying that, sweeping away all the things we needed to know about sex and death (seduction and putrefaction and sin and the wages of it) as fast as they could into a common grave. Among other things they laundered naughty songs, and many a jolt our grandmothers got when my friends and I would begin singing something like "A Guy Is A Guy," which with its original words had evidently been rather a dirty song in their own youths. But we had moved into the period that took the jolly, wordless rhythm of upstairs sex in "The Chandler's Shop" and made it represent the object, amusingly too horrific to name, found in a box on the beach—"The Thing." "Don't *ever* stop and open it up!" the narrator advises about mysterious boxes: if you do, you'll never be rid of it, boom-de-boom.

Some of us depended on horror comics, which before the federal cleaners caught up with them showed us the effects of the bed and the grave, one about as dire as the other. No wonder if Eros and Thanatos, those potent gods, appeared to have wound together in the dark like tree roots. Though we understood that horror comics focused on extraordinary cases, they were the most forthright paradigm of adult life that we had. EC, remembered as the best of the genre, were in their flamboyant last days cranking out tales of perfidy and revenge. Dangerous blondes with round breasts like anarchists' bombs, and curly-haired scoundrels with sinuous eyebrows, inspired, suggested, and perpetrated the murder of extraneous mates or business partners who later lurched back from their graves shedding gobbets of bruise-colored flesh. In one memorable story a murdered circus performer comes back on her murdered elephant and flattens the adulterers under two tons of putrefaction. Death was everywhere.

Our grammar school, where seventh and eighth graders struggled to puberty, sat in the field beside the Baptist cemetery, its own memento mori. Behind us the long wall of windows offered grass and graves, panoramic death. Seventh graders sat on the left side next to the attached outhouses, drafty passageways diluting the stench a little. Eighth graders, in the more desirable seats near the exit, had changed since we'd last shared a room with them. They looked closer to grown now, the girls wearing lipstick, the boys clumping in jumbo barn boots. They were allowed to wear class rings, to study Maine History and simple equations; they would have a graduation ceremony in June. Flirting at recess and noon hour, they pressed side against side on the fold-down seats. We didn't look as good as they did, but we could measure ourselves by them and hope that we had a future. Some, of course, had changed more than others. Simone, who (though defective only in effort, not wits) had repeated grades twice, looked as old as high-school girls, and in fact was. The eighth-grade authority on passion, she was going steady with a high-school sophomore, Robert. Her dark eyes, opaque as buttons, held back secrets.

It was well that our peers were entertaining, for our official resources were few and peculiar. For instance, that year the Maine State Library had loaned us a crate of books, dull volumes of instruction masquerading as fiction. They were full of pioneer children, and foreigners intent on raising flax. What did the State Library take us for? These books were beyond the piety of even my friend Elaine, who was devoted to the evangelizing romances of Grace Livingston Hill. As for me, Poe, though permitted, felt so illicit that he titillated me in a degree almost sexual and made every other writer dull as sugarless oatmeal. Lenore, lying on her drear and rigid bier, introduced me to such orgiastic, operatic degrees of remorse, bitterness, and grief that I hardly knew whether I was the corpse, or her lover, or the slanderous crowd, and I wasn't sure I dared to find out.

Gloria and I, who had once waited together for the Apocalypse, began now to school ourselves in movie-star data, not because we were stage-struck or indeed got to the movies more than once or twice a year, but because we required beautiful women to emulate, and our mothers, with their corsets and partial plates and housedresses, were no use to us. Between their condition at forty and our ambition at twelve no bridge could be imagined. We yearned after images of crystal and rose petal: Elizabeth Taylor, then in her exquisite twenties, was a peak of perfection so moving to me that I could ignore my own bookish, sloppy nature to suppose that I wanted nothing more from life than to look exactly like her. And what would I have done with such fire power? Fallen in love with myself, perhaps, and consumed to ashes.

I had been, as well, soothing my desperation that year by drawing cutaway buried-alive pictures in my school notebook (the visual influence EC comic covers; the conceptual, Poe; the emotional, puberty)— shrouded figures in their coffins, beating on the lids for exit. Sometimes I let them out—hollow-eyed, long-haired women, though occasionally men, staggering across the lined pages, free but not happy, like Madeline Usher. I could imagine their futures no more than my own. One day I showed the sketches to Gloria, who was likewise moved and eager for expansion.

Soon the Baptist cemetery found us singing through

clods of earth in Eddie Fisher's cupped, echoing hands; we could see him scratched and bloody but ravenous for some obscure satisfaction. Nor did Gloria's Marilyn Monroe (then ten years from her own grave and seeming immortal) ever fail to delight me, slinking seductively through the dry leaves, falling over her trailing cerements. The straight skirts of that year had taught us to walk in grave cloths. Elizabeth Taylor, revenant, blinked her lovely violet eyes at the confusing light, having awakened from a catatonic trance just in time. (Some things, I felt, you had to keep clean.) Life. Death. Exotic complications.

Thus Gloria and I took the edge off our unrest and filled in that awkward time until our new lives arrived. Others chose different forms of time filling: Simone, our trend-setting eighth-grader with the high-school boyfriend (Robert, of whom she was vastly proud), indulged in a kind of romantic merchandising, boyfriends' names on alphabet macaroni instead of "Jesus Saves," which she'd learned to make in Bible Camp one summer and now offered for twenty-five cents. It was an offer to be like her, perhaps, though awkward, as two seventh-graders claimed the same boy. Her eyes in those days, when she bragged of Robert, were proud and merry beyond our comprehension. She led us past crushed places in the tall grass, but Gloria and I didn't altogether get it. We weren't impressed. What did she want from us? She laid her head on her desk as winter passed but we hardly noticed. We were barely suspicious when she threw up in the outhouse passageway one morning, because who wouldn't?

In March we went, in a body, to Simone's wedding. Didn't dare wait till after graduation, said Gloria, or they'd have needed an extra mortarboard. Gloria and I added it to her repertoire briefly, Simone bulging through the diploma line, the child piping up from her womb like Jesus in "The Cherry Tree Carol." But we who had played zestful games of burial alive found Simone's situation too horrible to contemplate. It wasn't what she'd done to get pregnant that dismayed us, as much as how her games had caught up with her. Adult life had seemed comfortably far off, though the teens promised and allured. We were still young enough to think without reference to present talent that we might be famous singers or win Olympic medals, for we expected to be, when we were older, entirely different people. Perhaps it would fall to our lot to be exciting ones. How could Simone's future have arrived already and be so dull?

From my other side Elaine leaned over to say, "My mother talked to Robert's aunt. She says he cried all night when they told him he had to quit school and get married. He wanted to graduate and go to Ag school and now he never, never can."

"Never, never" was not a unit we knew how to measure, but we knew it was true, if you fell out of the system in those days, you were lost. Gloria was twisting her gloves. For the first time we felt ourselves ladies at the wedding of a contemporary and we were, in fact, depressed as hell. The rest of us had never pledged ourselves to anything but the flag, which didn't seem so far to expect much of us. Vows to Robert, with his human needs, weighed like anchors. This, and then the end? Was that how it went?

The rest of us were beginning and Simone was ending, Robert was over? Simone, who felt queasy, sat on a chair as far from the wedding cake as she could get. When Robert, left to himself, tried to horse with his high-school buddies, they acted as stiff and embarrassed as if the minister meant to play with them.

The familiar linking of sex and death, it seemed, might own a sort of metaphoric truth. We sat on cold folding chairs with our knees pressed together and contemplated the lost Simone. Her erotic trail blazing had cut a detour (which we might, but for the grace of God, have taken) past all the part of life we lusted for, leading her straight from girlhood to the tears and sleet of this wedding day. In her future no resurrections could be expected, but come summer the new generation would claw its way to the light, bloody and ravenous as Eddie Fisher.

Room

(1)

I'm fifteen and I no longer like going up to the lake. I object to it very much, in fact. Home isn't so good either, in the summer, with all my friends at the academy away, but at least there's the Post Office, at least there' s General Electric Theatre. Plumbing. When we start north to our camp I feel as though my arms are clinging to the back-door frame, stretching longer and longer. When my elbows pop and my fingernails tear away, my parents will just smile kindly and keep on driving. They find teenage angst endearing. What if a letter comes and I'm not home to get it? What if one of my friends needs me—goes into the hospital and wants visitors, has an emotional crisis and tries to phone our empty house?

My parents and Murphy and I are sitting in a little restaurant now, halfway to exile. My father and brother love it, they're impressed at the size of the servings, at the mountains of French fries, at gravy bulging and lolloping down the high sides of chicken sandwiches. The only reason I'm not anorexic is that in 1956 I'm unacquainted with that option. No, what I mind is physicality itself, the vulgar impetus to eat and excrete and breed and die. Maybe I can't thwart it by picking at a cheese sandwich, but I can take sides.

When my father gives me, as he always kindly does, a quarter for the juke box, I play "Unchained Melody," which briefly externalizes and purges my chronic, undirected yearning. *Time goes by so slowly, and time can do so much.*

At camp, outdoors is better than indoors, is closer to free. Just out of sight of the windows there's a loaf-shaped granite boulder on the shore. I know the toe holds and get up easily. Murphy is still too small to climb it, and my parents aren't interested. Up there I spend hours just watching the sun strike stars off the ripples and losing myself in dazzle. The rock's back is solid and warm as flesh, homely with freckles of quartz and mica. Its patches of gray lichen rest my eyes. Its immobility rests my spirits. This aspect of camp is excellent.

But sometimes I feel so lazy that I don't get any farther than the swing that hangs from two skinny trees beside the icehouse. I poke their sap blisters, leave moon-shaped scars. Under its gray skin the bark is the color of cinnamon. My heels drag. The seat was lowered for Murphy, who sometimes wanders by shyly for idle talk, lowering me too. We talk about how it will be when he begins school, what he'll have in his pencil box. It's a sleepy, soothing conversation spiced by the scent of resin. Nobody, least of all Murphy himself, would mistake me for the maternal flavor of sister, but my interest in the conversation is genuine, if slack: the litany of pencils and crayons and erasers still pleases. What's that about?

What's any of it about? In my room upstairs, my room without a real door, just a curtain, the iron bed, the back-painted mirror, call up the past but aren't strong enough to carry me there, nor are Osgood's cast-off magazines from the late Thirties, though I sit cross-legged on the bed and read them until their dress styles and pink-toothbrush remedy and use of Listerine for dandruff are familiar to me as Levis and hair dryers and Noxema. At the same time, my aesthetic improvements have failed to make the room modern or, for the matter, adult. I've tacked up *Time Magazine* ads for the Container Corporation, futuristic designs—stained-glass spirals, single black stalks of wheat—that tease me with their promise of a world I can only hope for. But I've undercut my own efforts, for although Murphy now has my collection of souvenir pennants, I have hung onto the calendar picture of the spaniel pups, childhood favorites whose names (Honey and Ginger and Clover and Cookie) my mother used for chanting me to sleep. I still have county-fair souvenirs of plaster and glitter, feathers and celluloid. Pulled here, leaning there, I pace in the starved, unseemly, throbbing present.

Nights, I curl up in the valley where my mattress swags, hugging my school sweatshirt, my prayers an inventory of people about whom I would, please God, enjoy dreaming. Sometimes instead I dream about spiders, dream that I walk into camp after a winter away and find so many on the ceiling that there's no place to stand without one over my head. Boat spiders, water spiders, outhouse spiders— spiders everywhere. In my dread I imagine more categories—tree spiders, rock spiders, shoe spiders. I scan all these places and more. I sometimes burst into nervous tears under the compulsion to watch all the ceiling and walls at once.

I used at least to imagine that I knew what I wanted. This object or that, to make my life completely happy. In the corner of the room there's an inflated plastic swan that reminds me of a thousand disappointments, spy cameras for which no film could be got, rainbow suckers with no flavor. In Woolworth's five years ago that swan looked ready to carry me through the waves all day on its white and graceful back. In fact it floated only on its side and refused to be mounted. I begin to suspect that there are no tools for walking on water, leaping ten feet in the air, seeing around corners.

That doesn't make the yearning quit. When I stand by my bed and dry off from swimming I'm sometimes pierced by a longing like knives, but I don't know what I want. I try to placate it with one thing and another. It's watermelon, I think, but when I hold a piece in my hand I know that's not it. Watermelon is not the name of what I long for, nor spiders the incarnations of what I dread.

(2)

For me, at sixteen, my room is the solid heart of home. Haven, hideout, study, dressing room, repository, salon. Mine, God bless it, Mine. The rest of the house has colored walls and white woodwork. The green woodwork and white walls of my room reverse this convention. I have learned that out in the world where I mean to go, people have white walls so they can Hang Art. I have hung art, a Feininger cathedral in a ready-made frame that almost fits it. I found the print in a bookstore. The family is polite but they don't understand abstraction. They understand

Maxfield Parrish, whom I like well enough but who does not advance my entry into the outside world.

Closet. My mother says it appears to be on fire; she's laughing because it's full of reds, pinks, yellows. I'm laughing too because already I've got one beige dress and one black plaid, signs of what I mean to wear when I'm older, to show that I'm older—my closet will be full of those charred neutrals when the hot roses of my earlier teens have grayed themselves out. I've stayed the same size for four years, so for the first time in my life I can accumulate. That's eight skirts! Already I can stand at the open closet door and feel a sense of accomplishment, a foretaste of how adults get a houseful of stuff.

I've put Dad's old tennis racquet in the back. Lately it's become clear to me that I won't play Wimbledon, since I hit the ball so seldom that I don't even want my friends to see me trying. My baton is in there with it, a heavy silver metal tube with white rubber balls on either end. Why do I have it? Who knows? In the late Fifties, every girl is a closet majorette.

Bureau. Low, wide, of thick, heavy maple, highly polished. Formerly my parents' set; full of cool, serious air and the scent of fancy soap. On top of it there's a little plastic-framed picture of Jesus. I got it in fifth-grade Sunday School and it looks like I've got it forever, because how can you not have your picture of Jesus up? What would I be saying if I put it away? I can't bring myself to make that gesture. I keep the little Steiff animals, tiger and owl and camel, in the opposite corner so the juxtapositions won't be so grotesque. It's the best I can do. In the middle my jewelry box offers friends a look, not for bragging but for intimacy

(3)

I'm seventeen, my friend is dead, and I'm visiting his parents. This is the first house outside the family that I've ever known intimately. Live-in intimate, I mean, knowing where the floor creaks and which doors need to propped with a rock, and what time of day the sink fills up with glasses and ash trays. It's an emptier house than ours, not so padded with domestic bric-a-brac, and it feels less safe. When the wind off the ocean blows the curtains straight in, nothing falls off the windowsills and nothing stops it.

His mother wrote to tell me that she hadn't had a proper chance to speak to me at his services, that she knew we'd been close and he would certainly want her to assure me that their home was always open to me. Could I perhaps spare them a week or so before I left for college?

I thought that there was nothing I would so willingly part withal, as Hamlet says, except my life, except my life, except my life. Freda Harrington's letter gave me hope that there were still things to want. My mother bought me two pairs of Bermuda shorts and I packed my suitcase with no quiver of misgiving about joining a household in crisis. I only knew that I was going to a place where nobody, probably, would be annoyed with my own grief or think I should snap out of it.

If I'd come here when I still saw the world as safe, would the coast feel different? Now it makes me think of people leaving, sailors and travelers. I look at the tides and remember that houses rise and fall and generations renew, that flux is nature's habit.

When I arrived, my hostess was sitting cross-legged on the kitchen floor, whacking the top of a Mason jar with a screwdriver handle. She was wearing pedal pushers and smoking. I hoped that my father, who had always told me with apparent conviction that nice girls don't smoke, wouldn't be shocked and haul me home. Freda Harrington looked like a different style of mother, no sign of girdles or aprons. I wanted, at once, to know more of her.

She took my father's hand with cries of gratitude—"Mr. Ireland, we so appreciate your lending us your precious Alice!"—and wrapped me in a soft, smoky hug. I was hardly aware of his driving away as, gazing, I followed her up the uncarpeted stairs to my room, where I lingered to absorb and unpack. Quite different from home, and yet it felt easy here. The woodwork was dark, the papered walls plain, a nautilus shell on the cedar chest the only ornament. Fog was rolling in already, but the view, I could tell, would be stunning.

I spend most of my time with Mrs. Harrington, Freda, which is fine with me. The rest of the family attracts me as well—a daughter who's closest to me in age, the son who looks most like my lost friend, the father who says he'll take me out pulling lobster pots. But she's the one who has brought me here and will, or will not, bring me again.

I try to help her in the kitchen. I love the slap-dash of this woman's housework. She's the first person I've known who leaves the clean dishes in the rack to dry. So you can do that, can you, I say to myself. That's a kind of liberation. Of course the dishes don't stay wet forever; her way makes sense. The other day, canning for the cat, she got tired of cutting up fish and began to shove them into the jar whole—heads, tails, fins, and all. I teased her about it, but I think that I may keep house that way myself someday. It appears to save time for other stuff.

What we do with the hours saved by domestic slapdash, my father would have with disapproval call "running the roads." These rides are meant to show me the scenery, which they do, but we drive every day like people running from something, which we are, though it doesn't work. We shoot up and down amazing hills, whip around curves known only to natives, and at every turn magnificence lays itself out in coves and island, sails and gulls. The world, now that I see a bit of it, seems sad but astonishing lovely.

Ordinarily we stop at the cemetery just before we go home, and whatever chat and joking we've managed goes silent. I'm as awkward as a dog in a suit. My friend, I know, is under my feet, I saw him put there, but how is that possible? And what am I supposed to do about Freda Harrington, on her knees now and weeping into the grass? Reaching out to hold her is the first gesture of my adult life.

On clear nights I roll my shades back up and get into my bed by feel, the economy of the dead, my legs together and my arms tight to my sides, but soon I slip, absent-minded, into the sprawl of the living. The blackness outside the window is the darkness of ocean and infinite space, not the darkness of the grave. There is more room out there than I know what to do with, but I believe, because I am here in this second home, that I will be able to occupy some piece of it.

Quiet Girls 1960

Carrie and I gaped from the door of our freshman dorm room: the sophomores and juniors had arrived. They greeted one another with rapturous cries, launching themselves shrieking into one another's arms. We'd never in all our rural Maine lives seen such an emotional display. And that was only the start. Orientation hadn't half told us. Waiting in line for lunch, the girls knitted, instinctual as silkworms, complex designs dropping from their needles while they chatted. After dinner they played bridge, sitting in fierce knots on the corridor floor and snubbing passersby. They sang songs about train toilets; they wore pearl earrings with their flannel pajamas. We made fun of their customs but we were nervous enough to adjust our hems and examine our pores. These girls appeared never to have had acne.

When one Friday after girls' curfew I heard an excitement of feet in the corridor I braced myself for another folkway. A panty raid perhaps? My mother had told me about those, another reason besides auto accidents to own good underwear. But there was singing now, coming closer— "Where oh where is Mitzi Morris? Way up high!" Carrie burst through the door with a crowd of our elders who without any greeting scrambled onto her desk and hung out the top of our window, just over the front doors.

"What is it?" I asked Scotty Frazier, a sophomore from down the hall. Her hair was still bleached from a summer's sailing.

"Mitzi's pinned," she said, pulling me nearer the window with a big-sisterly arm. "Shh. The boys are going to sing. It's a Theta pinning. They're the best; you're lucky this is your first."

Down on the cool grass, young men in chinos and loafers drifted towards the steps, crewcuts glinting in the floodlights. They were undeniably pretty, those college boys, and Scotty was right, they could sing. Their songs, golden and husky with longing, rose to the window, pleading for gentle girls who would worship them all their days. On that night I heard for the first time the solo that moved every bosom at Aubrey College to aspiration or despair: "I love a quiet girl . . . Warm as sunlight, soft as snow." A comforting girl, a clairvoyant girl—"She sees, she knows."

"Those are not quiet girls," I said to Carrie afterwards. "Those are girls who have already taught us thirty-seven synonyms for throwing up."

"I don't care," Carrie said with sudden fierceness. "I can be like them, I'll get pinned before I'm twenty, you wait and see, and I'm getting a rich man."

"Whether you love him or not?" I asked.

"I'll love him," she said between her teeth. "Mitzi's house has six bathrooms." Narrowing her green eyes she hitched up her skirt and danced around the room singing, "Jesus keeps him money in the Chase Manhattan Bank, Jesus saves Jesus saves Jesus saves!"

I was halfway scandalized and halfway amused, but mostly embarrassed that Carrie had heard of the Chase Manhattan Bank and I hadn't. "Where'd you learn that?" I asked.

"Oh, *everybody* knows that," she said, tilting her chin up like Mitzi.

If I had supposed Carrie's vow to be a passing impulse, I was wrong. Inside our closet door she taped a chart of eligible men subdivided by fraternities, little boxes waiting for scores in such categories as wealth, looks, manners, humor, brains. A check in the last box, "beast," meant that a candidate was better dropped unless very rich indeed. She went about dating and chart keeping with cold-blooded intensity, her calendar cross-hatched with engagements. I soon looked forward to her coming in and grading the latest date and would put aside Milton or Mill to watch her entrance. "Beast!" she might cry, tearing off her clothes as she raced around the room looking for her pen. Or she might stroll in like a bored debutante, to report, "Amusing but lacks polish," or she might come in as the Carrie I knew, thumbs up and grinning at a hot prospect.

We both understood that this shopping of hers was risky, ramping up the perils of the courtship games we'd been coached to play. Those shining, melodious boys didn't just want a quiet girl, they wanted snatch, they wanted pussy, they wanted to run through the night and howl at the moon. In the spring the Sigmas got out their big fishing net and immobilized girls in front of the Men's Union, rolling them until they were hysterical and stained with grasses. Walking down fraternity row to the bookstore was hazardous, as both the Alphas and the Epsilons threw water by the bucketful out of their upper windows onto passing females. The falling water struck a blow surprising in its weight; the cling of wet fabric violated the privacy of our bodies.

There were less metaphoric dangers as well. One girl on our floor went home pregnant, and the terrified whisper was that he hadn't even had it in her: the fierce, ambitious, high-jumping sperm had undone her. Hard not to be superstitious in the face of news like that, hard not to imagine sperm as tiny frat boys, jocular but ruthless; or, conversely, frat boys as wily, crew-cut sperm past whom we dashed, hiding our eggs as well as we could.

Carrie was braving the dangers, though. And if she wasn't quite like those tanned girls from six-bathroom houses, she was working so hard to pass that they forgave her. Their friendliness was not a ruse; life had nurtured them in kindness. She would be offered, and take, a second-semester bid from a sorority, though she had once laughed with me about the foolishness of the rushing teas.

As for me, I spent the fall waffling between lives. Couldn't I, like Carrie, aspire to be someone's Quiet Girl? I too had friends among the clean and knitting. The position they occupied in college I had, on a less pretentious plane, occupied in high school. I might muster the energy to catch up and start again. My clothes were okay. The silliness, though, would be hard to manage.

But at the same time I was lured by the songs of bohemia; I had signed up to learn backstage skills with the drama club. There boys and girl hunkered down together and plunged their hands into rusty buckets of set paint, rubbing it between their fingers to assess glue content with the casual skill of my grandmother tapping bread for doneness. They made witty allusions without smiling and wore work shirts smeared with grease paint (Fair Female, Sallow Old Man). They feigned inscrutability.

A black-haired senior called Lot spent his idle moments sitting on a pile of risers with a guitar, practicing, singing under his breath. The mysterious image of his first line, which I heard as "Like a rose upon the shore, Hallelujah," got into my head and seemed to me, after a while, to be about these people and yes, about me. Wasn't I like a rose upon the shore myself? Transplanted? Out of place? On the edge of the unknown? Sometimes the others would join in. This song was as familiar to all of them as kitting patterns to Carrie's new friends. "The River Jordan is muddy and wide," they harmonized. "Milk and honey on the other side." Better this promise, surely, than Jesus handing in his deposit slip at the Chase Manhattan Bank. I had supposed that I must be a Quiet Girl, well or ill, not dreaming of an end run around the whole field.

"Those people are weird and grungy," Carrie warned. "You won't get anywhere hanging around with the likes of them."

I knew they were weird—it was part of their attraction. As for getting anywhere, I thought if I would navigate that wide river I would probably like the other side better than Scarsdale.

"They're okay," I said. "You just don't know them."

"None of the girls are even pretty," Carrie objected, painting her nails a second coat of Tidewater Rose.

"Felicity Hale is very pretty," I said. "She's been engaged twice."

"Felicity Hale is just an *actress*," said Carrie, though I couldn't see how that disqualified her. "Cute, at best, if you don't mind freckles."

We didn't mind freckles—I was now thinking "we"—and found Felicity's charm and piquancy far more alluring than the soft nursery pinkness extolled in pinning songs. I adored this new, free life and bought a black jersey and some tight purple pants with little green Egyptians, suitable for cast parties, where everyone necked in a spirit of glad democracy.

One day, of course, I made out the real words to Lot's song, not a mysterious rose upon the shore after all, only "Michael, row the boat ashore." By then it didn't matter. I was already on the other side, replete with milk and honey, crying Hallelujah every day of my life for my deliverance. I hadn't understood before how convention could slap you flat with its weight, like a bucket of water thrown from fraternity row.

Once the sorting was over and we'd settled into our right places, Carrie and I stopped being edgy. Only the choosing had seemed adversarial. Girls in dorms, after all, kept the same hours, washed in the same basins, laughed at the same jokes. And there were other bridges. Many of us longed for, indeed lusted after, our male professors. They had already solidified, their features had definition, with them there would be no suspense, no changing of life course, no surprise at what faces would emerge from the matrix of undergraduate flesh. Moreover, they didn't seem to want quiet girls. They preferred us to say things: critical thinking, wit, even a bit of cheekiness was desirable. From the safe distance of their podiums, waggling their eyebrows, flirting, they cried to us, "Come, Madam, come! All rest my powers defie! Until I labour, I in labour lie!" And we understood the nuances to that image, for they had tutored us in six centuries of bawdry. We rose to it chirping. "Intellectual orgasms," said Felicity. At their direction we pursued phallic images through the ages, so much more civilized than being pursued through parking lots by the organs of our peers, which after all were only dicks, not phalluses. Did we believe on some level that our professors had metaphors in their own trousers? Possibly. "Perdition catch my soul but I do love thee!" they vowed. "Think of me, Sweet, when alone!" they begged. And indeed we did. They were our Mr. Rochesters, seasoned men and powerful. Were they perhaps attractively vulnerable as well? Could there come a day when they would need us? How Jane Eyre's line resonated—"Reader, I married him."

There were annual occasions, too, like Winter Carnival, that brought our disparate social worlds together, though not, in fact, socially. Winter Carnival saw the production of not only fraternity and sorority snow sculptures but some light though worthy piece of drama that attracted into its cast people with whom we did not ordinarily mingle and who disarmed us with their talent. Through all the weeks of rehearsal we would work together with a kind of delicate rapprochement like the cautious lifting of the heart that happens when a strange animal comes to be petted. After the play the alliance was over, though we sometimes smiled and waved regretfully when we passed each other on campus.

In the winter of my Junior year, long after Carrie and I had gone our ways, the drama club did Christopher Frye's

A Phoenix too Frequent, the tale of a Roman widow who decides not to die of grief in her husband's tomb after all, and Mitzi's roommate Jodi played the widow's servant who bursts from the tomb with the grand cry, "Ye gods, what a moon!" The theme of that Carnival was Fairy Tales, and though we made an annual point of ignoring the theme, we liked to think that *Phoenix* dealt with some of the same material (confinement, awakening, escape) in a less hackneyed way.

Each day as I crossed campus to work on the Roman tomb, I passed the sorority girls building snow sculptures of outsize female figures waiting for their princes—Snow White, Cinderella, Sleeping Beauty. That was what "fairy tale" had cued for the girls—the prospect of a happy ending, a romantic rescue. They were building themselves.

The boys, too, were building themselves, but not as the Prince Charming for whom the snow girls were waiting. Fraternity row exuded an air of misrule, Carnival with a more authentic flavor. In front of each house stood a stocky, blunt-headed, neckless dwarf, just humanoid enough to get away with it, just Disney enough for irony: their names stood before them in raised snow letters—Humpy, Horny, Cod.

"I think Snow White's stepmother was overanxious," I told Felicity as we passed that heroine's bulbous face. Sleeping Beauty, though, promised to be a triumph. She lay on her high couch with her virginal cheek against an up-flung arm, features clear as a looking glass, while her clothes grew daily more elaborate, iced and layered. We had begun stopping by the lacrosse field to admire her new buttons and ribbons, the classical drape of her skirt. Her makers were pleased and chatty.

The judges, who gave her, inevitably, First Prize, by-passed the priapic dwarfs with little shudders and gave the boys' prize to the Independents' Frog Prince. Maybe the dwarf makers were mad about that, or just full of testosterone and the phase of the moon; maybe they were enraged by Sleeping Beauty herself, a quiet girl without warmth, a girl whose snow was not soft at all but shielded with ice; or maybe they would have banged anything that couldn't get up. Coming back from class the week after Carnival, I saw a dozen girls around her snowy couch, pointing and waving their arms. I edged towards them cautiously. It might be none of my business, now that Carnival was through. But a dorm neighbor trotted over and pulled me back by my sleeve to show me the cracked ice around the hips, the smudge of wool fibers.

"What is it?" I asked. The marks made no sense to me.

"Hump marks!" said Jodi, outraged. "See where he had his knees? Somebody's been at her!"

"Gosh," I said, startled by the no-name sin, "What for?"

"Who the hell knows?" growled one of the girls. "Animals!"

"Beasts," I agreed, remembering Carrie's chart.

What could we do? Females were locked in at ten; males were creatures of the night. Each morning more girls gathered to observe with rage Sleeping Beauty's violation. Other changes began. Breasts that had once been delicate as Sleeping Beauty's face grew by nightly accruals into vulgar white cannon balls. I saw one girl raise her hand to knock them off, hesitate, and cross her arms over her own chest. Beauty's crotch was changing contour too, now that the ice had been breached: the snowy shield of her clothing was rubbed and molded until her skirts clung to her shape as though she'd been drenched.

Females looked with suspicion at male classmates: *What have you done in the dark?* There were rumors of break-ups and the handing back of pins, including Carrie's. When I looked her up and asked her about it, she could only say that she'd changed her mind, she wasn't ready. One senior English major tried to explain to her boyfriend that she didn't object to *him* but had suddenly developed an aversion to the phrase "being pinned." Male professors no longer met our eyes or enticed us with imagery.

Sleeping Beauty, the ultimate Quiet Girl, was never far out of our thoughts. She impressed her silence on us too. What the boys did at night we had either to acknowledge aloud during the day, which seemed compromising, or ignore, which was hard to do and seemed to drive them on. Perhaps there had been some point, earlier, when we could have knocked the sculpture down and been done with it, but that point seemed past. For any of us to break up Sleeping Beauty now would be self-injury.

On Friday morning of that long week Beauty was pinned to her pier by a toilet plunger, handle through the genitals. A sign wired to the cup said, "Wake Up, Baby!" The word at lunch was that Screaming Dot, the oldest and most fearsome of the gym teachers, had pulled it out and thrown it into the woods, and that she'd been crying when she did it. At any rate it was gone, and someone had been nurturing enough to pack the wound with snow.

Chapelgoers were the first to spread the Sunday morning outrage. They marched back to the dorms in their church hats and passed among the breakfast eaters like mildew, blighting the eggs with their murmurs of ritual defilement. Coats over pajamas, we crowded out to see and stood speechless before the final insult: there she lay crisscrossed and arabesqued with an illegible but clearly hostile yellow message about our futures, about what the boys intended in the ever after. Like the Quiet Girls of whom they had sung—and yet not like—we saw, we knew. For this was not the work of some passing thug, a solitary sicko, a random pervert. It had required a dozen bladders, fifteen, twenty—consensus.

That day there was no idle chatter. Girls stalked, cloaked in silent fury, to the library, where they studied in fierce silence. They averted their eyes from the lacrosse field, tightened their jaws. They moved in packs. When night fell they watched from windows.

At around two in the morning I felt a restlessness in the corridors and found myself putting on my coat. Though female students were not allowed out at night, not a housemother stirred to stop us when we propped open the outer door. Silent women passed from all their dorms to the lacrosse field. We must have looked like an old film, perhaps fifty dark figures working soundlessly against the shining white ground.

Reader, we buried her. Without discussion we scooped and rolled the snow from Beauty's field, all of it, laid it higher and wider over that silent sleeper, we who were awake. Long before the sky began to lighten, the winter grass was bare except for one great white heap. Shapeless. Featureless. Grotesque mammaries gone back to their elements, snow to snow, ice to ice. Lost in that tumulus the last yellow scribbles unformed themselves, powerless as dog piss.

"Ye gods," Mitzi Morris shouted as we raced back to our beds, "What a moon!"

What Song The Sirens Sang

The first taste of grown-up employment did not impress us, that was the consensus. My friends and I laughed and shared the tale of someone who'd risen up at his office and cried, "Bloody hell! I wish I was at University, if I was at University I'd go home!" Laughed but kept our own talismans safe in our emotional pockets, memories of some place where we'd felt more powerful. Mine was a weekend with Felicity and Lot in Greenwich Village, spring break of my senior year. The bright handful of days in that legendary place had promised a wider world. I'd read about Sam Kramer's shop with the brass hand for a doorknob, and there we were, palm on palm; I'd read Millay's poem about MacDougal Street, and now I stood there. Somewhere a steel drum was quickening my pulse.

I fingered that memory a little as I dined with my new colleagues, my first colleagues, at Miss Bealeigh's School for Girls. Just a quick, comforting vignette of me on Bleeker Street, blithe in the April sun, buying sandals with angular toes.

Now, in this nearly empty dining room, reflected light pooling on the French doors to the garden, I appeared to be the only person under fifty. Only the housemother and I were eating with our forks in our right hands. At college a few girls who'd done Junior Year Abroad ate left-handed, but I'd dismissed them as pretentious. My table mates did not appear to be pretentious, they appeared to be correct. Already I liked these people, yes, and admired them, foresaw that I might love them. The French master and his wife encouraged me to call them Andre and Charlotte and to join them for the opera broadcast. Mrs. Corticelli, the senior English mistress, who was now speaking of Zola in phrases so exquisitely constructed that they sounded like written English, had gripped my hands and pronounced me a lovely child. The Russian art mistress had turned my face to the light and called me "Poosy-cat," whereupon the housemother had, I thought, winked at me behind her back.

Later that night I sat on the edge of my bed, careful not to hit my head on the sloped ceiling. *Garret,* I thought, feeling rather Sara Crewe. But I was living in nothing worse than the maid's room in the top floor of a Victorian house converted to a dorm, and it seemed, in a way, an adventure. "An easy floor," Doris Sawyer, the second-floor teacher, had sniffed. "Only four girls." All the same I thought I'd be glad to trade my easy floor for hers, twelve girls but her own tiny bathroom and a real window. Worse, to compensate for her sniffing, she offered for my pleasure a look at the postcards she'd sent herself from the bus tours of thirty summers—not carried home, sent: *Dear Doris, thinking of you from Springfield, Illinois. Tomb of the Great Emancipator.* I already preferred the housemother, who'd given me a jelly glass of sherry and explained that when the girls came back we'd put it in cups so it looked like tea. The sherry, which was new to me, made me dizzy, but not as dizzy as the prospect of Doris Sawyer's postcards.

I wanted to be a good teacher. I prayed to be a good teacher. I had laid aside my wilder clothes, stashed them in a bottom drawer, and was learning to trap my hair in a French Twist, a struggle guaranteed to give each day a cranky start. I could hardly wait to meet the girls, whom I hoped to nurture as my colleagues were nurturing me. I meant to be a better balanced Jean Brodie, a more socially adroit Mr. Chips. And yes, if that was what it took, I was willing to live in the room of some long-gone maid. Though, hunched there, I thought of Felicity's apartment with its crystal decanters, a station on a different highway.

Before long I had settled into Miss Bealeigh's seductively genteel customs and ceremonies, though I had not quite sorted out my generational standing. Though a mere half dozen years older than the seniors, I was officially a different kind of creature altogether, one for whom they were obliged to spring to their feet and open doors or carry books. Sometimes I forgot and let them bitch about the headmistress, Miss Vickers; sometimes they forgot and made me wear my rain coat, or scolded me into bed when I had a bad cold. They were pleased that I still carried my books in a green Harvard bookbag, unable yet to embrace the awful adulthood of a briefcase. Though I secretly preferred the bad girls, the schemers and cussers and smokers-in-bed, I tried to remember that the campus leaders were now my allies, no longer my natural adversaries. In fact, though both sorts were rather more sophisticated than I—they spoke casually of Paris, they taught me to hunt for the Nina in a Hirschfeld drawing—they were still dewy and vulnerable and sometimes, to their humiliation, slipped and called one of us "Mom." I loved the work, exhausted in my skinny bed I fell asleep every night loving it.

My colleagues, thirty or forty years older than I, were my official peers. I was flattered by this supposition, I aspired, but some emulations were still beyond me. For instance, I could no more carry a serious purse than I could a briefcase: several times that year I bought promising handbags but passed them on to my mother, for whom they seemed better suited. I had hopes for the bag that had a kind of Esme Corticelli look, but in the end it merely became my mother's favorite. These colleagues were my mother's generation, with children my age. Their raptures at prospective visits from grown daughters were rather an eye-opener.

"I thought my folks were excited to see me because their lives were so dull in that pokey town," I admitted. "I thought I was like an envoy from the outside world."

They laughed at me in chorus, surprised and indulgent.

"Nothing to do with it, my dear!" Mrs. Corticelli said. "Believe me, it's your own too cute self they're pining for!" She gave my chin an affectionate pinch.

Charlotte and Andre Loriot became my closest friends. In those precious gaps between classes and meetings, meetings and evening supervisions, I could climb three flights and knock on their little door; it sat plumb with the edge of the top step, no landing, which made their apartment seem like a treehouse. Behind that door their life was marked by modest pleasures, hard to come by, worth sharing with friends. I learned to eat artichokes there and fondue. Sometimes we'd run away to a film together, or go for long rides, pooling pocket change to see if we could afford supper out, as though we were college students again. It was good.

The widows managed on even less than Charlotte and Andre. Lily Holiday laughed and contrived out of odds and ends a house of enormous charm—painted junkshop frames for coffee tables, cheap dolls, bookcases full of fancy second-hand editions. The Russian art mistress paid homage to an earlier, wealthier life by decorating holiday mantelpieces with fake gems, tinsel, glitter and gilt. Chin up in every sense, old Mrs. Concord, who lived in a tiny apartment crammed with family furniture, wore a child's sash for a muffler.

One evening Charlotte and Andre began to instruct me in school politics, to take me farther in, lower down. They thought it fair, they said, to tell me right away that I might damage myself by being their friend, for the headmistress was out to undo them.

"What for?" I asked in amazement. She was hiring so much virtue for so little money.

"She hates everyone who knew the founders," said Charlotte. "Vicious old tart."

"Now, now," said Andre.

"Miss Beatrice and Miss Aurora Leigh would have a fit if they could see their school today," mourned Charlotte.

"But it's marvelous," I objected. "It's a perfectly enchanting school." Only that morning I had listened to the girls' chorus practicing "For All the Saints" in their sweet, ethereal voices. I thought of the back garden, where students could pick flowers for their rooms, and of evening prayer in the senior dorm. I was in love with the place.

"You can still feel it?" Charlotte cried.

"We thought it was dead," said Andre.

They seemed close to tears. After that moment of intimacy they led me deeper into the school psyche –showed me a place of clandestine foes and secret wounds, machinations too subtle for the uninstructed eye. It was the underside of that intensely female world, so attractive on its surface, with only self-deprecating Andre to counter sensibility's undertow. This revelation did not make the surface of school life less engaging. Quite the contrary: it seemed possible that one's career could be well spent in maintaining the enchantment.

The news about Miss Vickers was a blow, though, for I had a natural hope of being liked by my employer. But after all, her favor was nothing beside my loyalty to the Loriots. Now that I knew, I could see that she was indeed tormenting some of my frailer colleagues, and Charlotte told me that she had driven my predecessor into early retirement. Brutal class loads, cramped rooms, cold shoulders—headmistresses have an arsenal.

Even Miss Vickers' readings in morning chapel revealed themselves as hostile now. "Let them be confounded and consumed that are adversaries to my soul," she would intone. "Let them be covered with reproach and dishonor that seek my hurt." And it was true, the faculty, those sweet ladies, did wish to eat up her flesh and cast her into a pit and take away her life. I would watch their faces as she declaimed, "Give them according to their deeds, and according to the wickedness of their endeavors: give them after the work of their hands; render to them their desert!"

On the rare weekends when I was off dorm duty and had no obligations to school activities, I would sometimes take the train to New York. Lot and Felicity's household was a restful counterpoint to the hormonal fen of Miss Bealeigh's. Whereas the school was fulminating with emotion thinly contained by courtesies, Lot was perfecting deep male inscrutability; his ideal was the possibly apocryphal coffee house audience that, too cool to clap, merely snapped its fingers. He reminded me of other options, other lives.

Back at school, as the long claustrophobic winter set in, Doris Sawyer began to fray. I had never sought her but now I dreaded her. The housemother and I drank sherry still as mice, hoping that Doris wouldn't notice us. "Did you like being married?" I asked her. "Is it worth doing?"

I was asking everyone about marital options in those days, hoping not to get it wrong myself. "Having the children was worth it," she said. "The marriage wasn't up to much. My husband ran off with a beautiful blonde. I'm not sorry I did it, but it isn't for everyone. Don't feel you have to."

When I left I'd try to drift by Doris's door, immortal, invisible, hid from her eyes, but she'd shoot out like a trapdoor spider and have me by the wrist, giving voice perhaps to some diatribe against students that was already playing in her head: "—no respect and their pettipants show, boys and dates, boys and dates, what do they are about the deaths in Boston-—."

Her special history topic for the year was the Boston Molasses Flood of 1919, that death-dealing January escape of nearly three million gallons of molasses from a holding tank near the harbor. She kept a mayonnaise jar half full of molasses on her bureau and would tilt it back and forth to give visitors an idea of its viscosity. "Roads sticky all the way to Worcester," she'd announce grimly, or "Children buried like flies in amber." No temptation to interview this one about how she found the single life, I could hardly bear to hear how she'd found her morning classes. Sometimes she'd whisper about Miss Vickers, pinching my wrist in her damp fingers. "A certain party moved my napkin to the wrong cubby. I had to wipe my lips with my handkerchief. What kind of example to the girls is that?

"Do you really think it was Miss Vickers?" I'd say blankly, taken each time by surprise, despite the Loriots' coaching, at the concept of intrigue so petty.

"Who else? The viper herself or that evil minion she calls a secretary."

"All the secretaries and staff were crying after lunch," I might offer, hoping to cheer her, "It seemed to be something about usurping one another's duties."

"Usurpation," she'd say darkly. "Even the workers are wretched, even the workers."

I turned to the Loriots for sympathy but found their sympathies largely with Doris.

"Oh yes," said Charlotte, unalarmed. "Doris always has the winter crazies, poor thing. They seem to be early this year."

"Winter crazies, how you talk," Andre chuckled. "Miss Beatrice would every winter send her a pound of English tea and Miss Aurora Leigh would send her a bottle of French brandy, they were very dear and patient. She will be better by March."

"But with Miss Vickers in the equation—," said Charlotte. "Don't you remember what happened last spring?"

"No need to tell it," said Andre, but Charlotte gave him a fond glance and went on.

"Mercy Baker said something so rude about old maids and Dust Bowls that Doris cried and left the room. Mercy told everyone that Doris had thrown a shoe at her and run out into the mud in her stocking feet."

"No!" I crowed.

"It was not so funny," said Andre. "What Mercy said was very hurtful. Doris said she would come back only when the class learned an Arlo Guthrie song and sang it for her. So Miss Vickers thought to fire her then, but Esme Corticelli went to bat for her. She said even a fool should see that Doris meant Woody Guthrie, perfectly good teaching material, and could Miss Vickers really suppose that she intended them to sing "Alice's Restaurant"? Miss Vickers, who speaks only English, can be intimidated by languages, and Esme was tri-lingual at her."

"Does Esme *like* Doris?" I asked, hoping not. Because if she saw something I'd have to try to see it too, and then I'd be trapped.

"Oh no," said Charlotte, "but she likes a little stir and she gets to go home when it's over."

"It was a very kind thing she did," said Andre.

"Kind hearts are more than coronets," said Charlotte with airy irrelevance. "Mercy Baker kept the shoe and says she's having it bronzed for a dust bowl."

On Wednesday afternoons I sometimes had tea with Lily Holiday. We tucked our feet up on her sofa and nibbled macaroons off a shared plate.

"Mad for coconut!" Lily murmured. "I suppose we

should ask that poor Doris to tea, but she's no fun these days."

"Was she ever fun?"

"Not much," Lily admitted, "but twenty years ago she could still laugh. She probably should have married. Maybe she'd have got somebody who'd listen. And be out of the dorm. Only single people get caught in the live-in trap."

"Could you have lived in?"

"Rather death," said Lily cheerfully. 'Talk about getting stuck in molasses! Miss Beatrice offered me the senior dorm when Chuck went, but I've got enough clothes to see me out and I don't eat much. I can pay the taxes if I'm careful and the creek don't rise."

"Really, I'm okay," she added, reading my eyes. "It's pretty lonesome sometimes, but friendship can keep you connected. If I can't sleep nights I get up and walk around till I find a spot. Imagine that in a dorm."

"Oh look, Girls, Mrs. Holiday's on the ping-pong table again," I imagined.

We giggled like sophomores.

"But be as kind to Doris as you can stand to be," she said. 'I imagine that it's terribly, terribly grim to be her."

Not many mornings later, Miss Vickers tapped my shoulder as we were putting away our napkins, and announced that she would see me upstairs in her office. (What had I done? Could I really be fired for loving the Loriots? What would my parents say?) Her feet beat doom on the uncarpeted stairs; she flung herself into her desk chair and began to page viciously through her leather-bound Bible, a kind of vicarious pacing. I waited. "Sit!" she snapped, as one might address a dog.

Sitting, I stared at the hem of my gray skirt, which might be too short, or on the other hand too long. I thought that she'd paged about as far as *Jeremiah*. Lots of good fierce passages there. "No, honestly, Miss Vickers," I thought about saying, "I haven't sat in the assembly of the mockers." But of course I had. At that very moment I was rehearsing the scene in my head for Charlotte and Andre.

"Yes, Miss Vickers?" I prompted. Better to get it over, whatever it was.

"Miss Ireland," she said, "Time for a talk about your progress. The girls seem fond of you—your youth attracts them, I suppose—though you must remember to maintain your distance. And you are making friends with the faculty, are you not?" Her courtesy seemed some beast on a choke chain.

"Yes," I admitted, thinking with affection of pooling change with Andre, of macaroons with Lily, of sherry in teacups. And if Esme Corticelli and I didn't spend much time together— she had a separate life of translation and review, for which she was chauffeured away after classes by a small, hot husband in a Fiat—we gravitated together at school events and laughed at one another's stories. We connected.

"You are too young to judge your elders wisely or see them clearly," Miss Vickers said with the start of a snarl, which she checked briefly to add, "You must know Doris Sawyer very well."

"Not very," I said cautiously.

"And why is that? Is she anti-social?"

"Oh no, quite social, but I find that I'm closer to some of the others."

"Indeed," said Miss Vickers, sucking the word like an acid drop, rolling my friends on her tongue. "But to return to the case of Miss Sawyer, I would appreciate your confidence. Does she seem to you quite—right?"

"About what?" I stalled. Doris Sawyer revolted me, but what Esme Corticelli saw fit to save I would not help to throw out. And Lily said I should be kind to her. The circle of nurturing had closed around her. Playing Red Rover I had always been the weak link that bullies ran at. Miss Vickers had sensed it. If I were at University, I'd go home.

Miss Vickers' thumb raced for the fires of Armageddon but she had no need to look down, they burned in her bosom. "Take care, Miss Ireland," she said. "You've been seen in her room. I have my sources."

What did she imagine I'd been doing there? Had someone heard Doris call her a viper? Had my smile looked too authentic? And who could mean to undo me? Not my girls! Not Millie the housemother!

"She shows me her postcards," I said, hating the squeak in my voice.

"Ah, *postcards,* said Miss Vickers, making a view of the Williamsburg stocks sound naughty and French.

But she had played with me long enough. Now she narrowed her eyes and pounced. "You've made mistakes," she said. "Quite a few of them. You've worn jeans in the dorm. You've made phone calls during Quiet Hour. You've let your table refuse hot cereal. But your big mistake is in trifling with me. You think you can side with the others and cover up for Doris Sawyer; you think they'll like you for it. But they aren't your friends, they won't cover up for you. They haven't. You don't know your friends from your enemies. The Loriots! Lily Holiday! You are an ignorant, reckless child. That will be all, Miss Ireland: get on with your—-work."

She didn't have to say "if you can call it that." Contemptuous question marks nipped and rattled in her tone like finger bones. The Bible lay dry on her desk. I could barely see.

I groped downstairs in a world gone viscous, my smile at the housemother's inquiring look a grimace. Swept into the morass of intrigue and suspicion that made secretaries weep and teachers retire early, I couldn't work my mouth. The Loriots had tried to teach me. I longed to tell them what Miss Vickers had said, but I'd stopped knowing who they were. They should be safe, if they were why she hated me. But that was what *they'd* said. And what if one was my friend and the other not? Even the gentle Andre could be hiding a contrary face.

Restless nights followed thin-skinned days.

"What's the matter?" said Charlotte.

"Can you not tell us?" begged Andre.

"I can't!" I wept. "I can't talk about it!" They plied me with solicitude and cake, but still I didn't dare.

"Someone giving you trouble?" asked the housemother darkly. I shook my head and fled to my garret.

"She'll undo us all!" cried Doris from her doorway.

Lily held her tongue and poured brandy in my tea.

Out of my depth and thrashing, only technically grown up, I'd had no idea adult lives got so complicated. I couldn't fathom their aims or guess their limits or make sense of alliances. The flatlands I had imagined between thirty and death were riddled with pits and tricks. Even so the children of Boston must have felt when the harmless molasses on their bread turned savage and had them on toast.

"Darling, you look a fright!" Esme Corticelli exclaimed when we met between buildings. "Female troubles?"

"Not the sort you mean," I said. It was the first moment of light, seeing and liking the ambivalence of that phrase. My mind working again, I cast myself, metaphorically, on her bosom. When I cried, "I need a confidante!" she seemed surprisingly pleased.

That afternoon at her house I laid out the whole soggy tangle, more free from it with every moment of her attentive gaze. Of course my friends were my friends; of course Miss Vickers was, as Doris said, a viper. I felt as though I'd just had a long shower and put on dry clothes. I'd been silly to bother this woman, but in her stringent company the air seemed fresh again. "I see now it was all foolishness," I said. "Sorry to have troubled you." I would go back to my life at school and in time find it idyllic again.

But Esme Corticelli was looking at me long and a little sadly. Then "Out," she said with decision, her amethyst ring flashing in the sun like the angel's fiery sword at the gates of Eden. "Get the hell out of here, Chickadee, while you can. I shall miss you, but Miss Bealeigh's is no place for someone like you."

"But I like it here," I protested. "The girls, and the ceremonies, and the tea parties. All those wild, wonderful ladies." *And you, Esme, I wanted to add, are the most elegant person I know. How do I learn it all if I leave?*

"The ladies," she said flatly, "are sirens. They'll sing

their spells and keep you here. This is all an enchantment, a charming ephemeral cobweb. You must see that."

Trying for just one moment longer not to see it, I offered an absurdity: "So Doris Sawyer's a siren?"

"Not a siren herself, but she listened. So you see."

I did see. I saw the bones of Doris Sawyer washed on the ocean floor. I saw my own.

She nodded, sharing my vision. "You could marry," she went on. "Or go back to graduate school. Both. Just get on with your life. You have a good brain and are moreover sufficiently attractive. As the Italians say, *Il contatore gira,* which means 'the meter is running.' Don't for godsake give up living at twenty-four."

The school was staffed by people with their pasts already earned, she meant; it was not for me a path to the future, with which I had an obligatory engagement. In that future there might or might not be amethysts or bylines or hot men in Fiats, but there would be unfettered hair and breezy sandals; and when I traveled I would send the ladies postcards from Cairo or Istanbul with my love, but I would never, now, be in danger of sending them to myself.

The House of Pride

"Ivory tower" has always held for me the sound of enchantment, never mind that it's tossed off with contempt. Ivory—the grain and glow of it, its curves and carviness. A whole tower of ivory, shining in the rarified air, it's the ultimate luxury, if you can keep your mind off the elephants. And towers, with their lovely, far-seeing isolation above the dust and tumult. Who would not dwell in ivory towers?

Having arrived in Toronto for grad school with eleven boxes of books and a headful of elitist agenda, I rented the closest thing to a tower I could find, a modest eighth-floor studio apartment set among ordinary houses. I sewed buck-a-yard drapes for the big window, set candlesticks on the table, and before long I was drifting around the room naked, looking down at the treetops, testing the powers of invisibility. What might not be possible in this new life?

On my first Sunday in that good city I dressed and headed downtown to Saint James, the Anglican Cathedral, in pursuit of holy days, orders of angels, church seasons with all their rites and colors and vestments. Having latched the pew door behind me and pressed my knee-caps against a little hinged plank of dark wood, I watched the procession of a male choir so refined that they seemed in danger of etherizing. "From battle and murder, and from sudden *death*," they chanted, their edged articulation giving "salvation" four syllables; the sweet, high note of "death" made sudden death seem after all a thing to be sought, not delivered from. In my childhood I had been moved by the special-occasion male quartet singing "My Anchor Holds" downstairs in the Baptist vestry. This choir moved me for opposite reasons: hearing them, it seemed possible that one might hoist anchor and fly off to glory, or whatever less fundamentalist thing than glory Anglicans fly off to. I was seeing and hearing things for which I had no names. I would learn them. The man with the wand: verger. The man in the morning coat: churchwarden.

"There's a woman screaming!" I whispered to the boy in the next pew.

"It's the descant," he said kindly.

At the University as well I was finding wonder at every turn. The society for medieval drama gave plays, admission free: under the rose windows of West Hall they crucified a young man with a dancer's body while the audience sat on the floor and wept. In Massey College the weather bulletin addressed the Western Wind, a number of professors still taught in academic gowns, and everyone's favorite newel post was a curled gryphon. I had been wanting this world all my life without knowing its name.

The heart of my academic experience, the class most challenging and least given to revealed assessment, was Professor Ruth Stewart's Coleridge seminar. Energy arced down the table from our professor's seat, deriving not only from scholarly eminence but from some inexpressible force of will. At our initial meeting she chewed, briefly, a corner of her lower lip, pieced us one by one with a bright hazel look, and announced that she did not care for the term "Romantic Movement," which seemed to her silly. There swept over us at once an encompassing shame that we had ever supposed "Romantic" a viable term, and a resolve not to seem silly in her class of all places on earth. Her firm, fine-boned hands, jotting assignments in a notebook, looked made for steering and hammering, possibly for steering and hammering us. We came out reeling. Forrest Connor (who fifteen years later would consider naming his child Samuel Taylor) looked thoughtfully at the toes of his moccasins and then up again. "If she weren't so old," he said at last, "I would divorce my wife and marry her." Nobody laughed.

We knew that we had hold of the real thing, or she had hold of us, and were soon bound to her by links of admiration, terror, awe, even a kind of love. Thus beyond a sensible wish to carry off an A, some of us conceived an even more ambitious desire to please her personally, to say that thing which would cause her eyes to warm with recognition of a kindred mind. In vain we brandished readings flavored with Freud or Bodkin. In vain we jigged and sweat, flashing tentative, hopeful smiles. When we finished speaking she would look at us with no readable expression and ask whether that was all, a question that appeared at the time not so much a neutral request for information as a complaint of inadequacy.

Only Forrest seemed undismayed. Although critically inclined to baroque complications, sometimes ignoring the surface of a work altogether, he dwelt in a kind of detachment that I admired and hoped some day to emulate. I had seen him unwrap layers of meaning with the same peaceful smile he wore peeling off the layers of winter, and though I was slow to believe it, he eschewed even academic competition, seeing it, perhaps, as a form of violence. He soon became my closest friend, which his wife seemed not to mind. I myself had achieved a small detachment but I hoped for more. For instance, having no money to speak of, I was fairly detached from any interest in clothes, though I did quite like the student-poverty look of uppers bound to soles with electrical tape.

Perhaps, too, my friendship with Forrest helped me by contrast to see absurdities. In the light of his rational affection I may have begun, sooner than I would have, to doubt whether what I'd taken to be necessary nuisances were necessary after after all. For instance, a person dated, that seemed to be a given, beginning as early as parents permitted and keeping on until what—until a match was made? Until marriage? What about people who didn't marry, then? I thought of the older unmarried women I knew, none of whom seemed to be dating. How had they known when to stop? There seemed to be no rules. I, who had been dating since my teens in a stolid, dutiful way, had never (save in passing flickers of passion) desired mating or marriage. I wanted freedom more than I wanted love. I was beginning sometimes to ask myself, "What am I doing?"

I ask it as I sit in my apartment, my Coleridge open on my desk, bickering with a weedy Englishman from church. When I tell him that I need to work on a report, and no, I don't want to cone over and give him a sloppy kiss, he complains that too much study isn't good for girls, it blunts their instincts.

I ask it as I sit on the library steps with a rather sweet student from Nairobi, who worries that I'm not on birth control. "What if someone falls in love with you?" he says. Later I see that he may mean himself, but all I can think at the time is that he's got it backwards: shouldn't it be what if I fall in love with someone?

I ask it when a guy I met in the elevator, who's just taken me to hear Howlin' Wolf, is making what seems to me a yawningly lame seduction ploy. "It would be a good way to get acquainted," he says. "You'll like it, everybody does. Haven't you heard about the sexual revolution? Just scratch my ears, will you?" As I try to make my hand go, politely, to these strange ears on this strange head on my personal, familiar lap, I reflect that I've heard the everybody-likes-it argument all my life, beginning with children's birthday parties, and have never once been impressed. It crosses my mind that I must have had the sexual editions of this conversation about a hundred times by now, except for the ear scratching. That if I ever have it again I may crack up and begin to yell. That I am, it seems, through dating, and isn't that a relief! I look at the face in my lap with something close to gratitude. My private sexual revolution appears to have moved counter clockwise.

General Exams were scheduled to start early in Lent, those fearsome tests wherein for the first and perhaps last time a candidate for dissertation writing must know everything about English and American Literature simultaneously and in detail. Forrest and I studied for five or six hours a day, argued, read aloud poems too soporific to handle alone. I came to my first Ash Wednesday service not only penitent but keyed up and worn out. I had no idea what to expect at the altar rail, where priests passed along the row of kneeling people, murmuring. One paused in front of me and pressed an ashy thumb to my forehead. "Remember, O Woman, that thou art dust and unto dust thou shalt return," he said gently, making it sound as intimate as a message from a lover, and more objective. The thought of my dust was oddly soothing. I could feel hanging between my eyebrows through the rest of the service the black smudge by which I was explicated, a thing worth remembering.

In April I gave my last seminar report for Professor Stewart, an analysis of the difference between the well-known published version of Coleridge's *Table Talk,* edited by his nephew and son-in-law Henry Nelson Coleridge, and the undoctored table talk in H.N.'s manuscript notes, which the college possessed thanks to Professor Stewart. I had hopes for it. While the first student droned on overtime I sketched him gagged by his flowered tie and wondered how I could bear to give up knowing Ruth Stewart. Impossible to grasp that a person with whom I was so visually familiar would go out of my world completely when the seminar was over. I knew, we all knew, the way her hair sprang back from her forehead and how she crossed her t's. The academic world mates and unmates us too casually, I thought. By now I was checking all my work against what I could grasp of her standards, asking myself sternly, *"Is it true? Is it clear? Is it necessary?"* She would always, likely, be in my mind to keep me straight, while I must assume that I had left no tracks at all on her mental terrain.

The student with the necktie wound to a slow close. He was twelve long minutes over his allotted time, and very boring he'd been. This was awkward, for we had no more class meetings into which we could run leftover episodes.

Professor Stewart checked her watch, then looked at the two of us who had reports still to give.

"We're running late," she observed. "Could either of you shorten your report?"

Silence. How could we afford to lose our last chance to impress and be rewarded? I was dying to give my *Table Talk* report with every single witty and sensitive judgement intact, hoping that this last time the fire of approbation would come down and consume the offering.

"Come now," she said, looking harried. "We've only so much time. Someone will have to help out."

She doesn't seem to understand, I thought, that she's asking one of us to damage ourselves. Then I thought, it would not be prudent, but it could be a gift. This is the last chance to please her. I can sacrifice my interest. And I heard myself clear my throat and say offhandedly, "I could shorten mine, I guess."

"Thank you," she said, giving me, straight into my eyes, the transfixing glance of recognition I'd been waiting for, like a silver nail.

I talked full tilt and didn't leave much out, after all, except some multiple illustrations. It was over in ten rattling minutes, the fastest seminar report on record.

"And why," she said, "do you suppose that H.N. changed the dates and redistributed the conversations?"

"I think maybe he wanted to look as though he'd been to dinner more often than he really had," I said, not a very academic answer.

"Yes," Ruth Stewart said, "that's astute of you."

Fulfilled, I basked briefly in Forrest's pleasure for me and the probable envy of our seminar mates.

"And now," she added briskly, "I suppose we'd better arrange for a final exam so that I have something on which to grade you."

Our jaws may have dropped in unison, but I was too poleaxed to check the others. She had never been grading the reports. The reports had never been showcases about us, about me, about student cleverness and industry. They had been about literature—only, and purely, about that. This was why she seemed not to notice us, why she asked always if there was anything more. Forest had been closest to understanding after all. I had behaved correctly only when, not knowing I was right, I had acted for love and not for profit.

Walking home across Queen's Park I stopped twice to drop onto benches and stare at the squirrels, who appeared to enjoy an unpretentious singleness of mind. At home I went straight to the sink and drank a glass of water for the clarity of it, looking at my National Portrait Gallery pictures of writers, hung like hunting trophies. Hung, I now felt, wrongheadedly, boastfully, with a kind of name-dropping. Stretching out on the futon, though I rarely lay down in the daytime, I fixed my eyes on the spring sky and drifted. On the edge of sleep there came to me a jolt of insight like Ash Wednesday's, not into the world's pettifogging squalor but my own. For one breathless moment I had a glimpse of myself as God might see me, grubby and wretched and raddled with sin—a flaw, a blemish, a surface imperfection on His mirror, which is the world. A blot through which Divine vision alone would be keen enough to catch any poor reflection of itself. But, though I would sometimes backslide, I was a flaw resolving now to reflect as lucidly as my nature permitted, without games or vanity, the necessary, the clear, and the true.

Between
the Funerals

It's my father's last upright summer, and my mother and Murphy are trying to grass him in, a gesture that in retrospect will take on implications until their practical, self-interested motives are almost consumed in symbolism. This battle of horticultural wills is taking place on the back half of our side lot, which by local custom is plowed up for planting. The half near the street is mowed, with a border of irises at the rear, a concession to living in town. But behind the flowers a quarter-acre of raw dirt says (in a voice like my father's, lightly jocular), "Drop the affectation and get over here with the fertilizer. We're still in the country." Vegetables raised on this quarter-acre can feed us all year, with leftovers to give away.

My mother and Murphy skulk and worry around the edges of the bare earth with bags of grass seed. They're damned if they plan to spend the summer nurturing a mess of surplus vegetation that my father is just barely strong enough to plant but clearly not strong enough to care for. But their plan, to start grassing on one end of the garden plot while he starts planting on the other, to meet him halfway and cut him off, has been countered by an unexpected move. Frail, shaky, and stubborn, my father stands in the *middle* of the garden, dropping dry peas into furrows, stopping to breathe and tuck nitroglycerin pills under his tongue. He is foxing them one last time by sowing his seed from the center out.

I feel some sneaking sympathy for my father, but self-interest is strong in me too. There has risen up a useful fiction that I'm too hopeless, lazy, and bookish to garden. I conceal, almost from myself, the sense of connectedness I feel between my bare feet and the warm dirt, which sometimes appears to throb. I hurry back, swatting at black flies, instead of burrowing my face into the tomato vines to breathe greenness. This is the summer I should rise above family myth, I know it, but a larger anxiety keeps me quiet, for just now power balances seem precarious and I dread to shift my weight.

My father's motives have been neither revealed nor discussed. Maybe he's bent on feeding us one more time. Maybe in the face of death he wants to raise a final, spectacular green tribute to life. Maybe he damned well won't be bossed while he can still stand up. Makes no real difference. In my family we've never heard of last wishes; with us, the dying lose their franchise early.

And maybe, of course, he's still the smartest of us and hears a message that the other two (now tentatively grassing from both sides) don't know they're sending: your place on earth is narrowing towards your grave; grass will cover you; our preferences will root and flourish; the country part of us is going under with you.

2

My mother has sold the land in Aroostook County, the 2500 acres my father accumulated to exorcise boyhood poverty. What did they mean to us, who hadn't been hungry in those fields? She got sick of neighbors calling long-distance to tattle: "So-and-so's cutting on your land." You can't blame her, Aroostook's not her heritage. She married the north, and now it's over; if the man is gone, let his baggage go too.

The situation's different for me, a little. One glance will tell you that paternal input dominates my genetic code. Old people near the farm sometimes forget and call me Gyp, seeing my aunt in my face. Murphy resembles my mother's side, excellent people and close to us, but I'm feeling a little isolated. When the pair of them throw out my father's packrat clutter, so like my own, I grieve and panic and fly into a defensive rage.

I couldn't quite bear, in the end, to have all that land go. Some atavistic homesteading instinct cried out that I could shelter on land, grow root vegetables, survive. When my mother managed to take in my incomprehensible plea—"Save me some land, save me some land!"—she deeded over a hundred acres of daisies and wild strawberries in the tall grass, and in the center, on top of a little rise, some family headstones. I have under my wing the bones of Auntie Gyp and Uncle Harris, of Lillian who died young, of my grandparents and great-grandparents.

Now we're selling the farm itself. Even I see that it should have been sold years ago, after Uncle Harris died. None of us want it. For me the life went out of it with Auntie Gyp; my mother never liked it. Murphy knew it only in decay. But my father couldn't let it go, it was the Home Place, a monument to his mother's energies. For him all those long early years that disproportionally fill our memories had been lived there, the births and deaths, the jokes and dinners and lessons, the views from windows. He tried to keep it lived in by cutting deals with the needy, but one family stole the silver and used the coffee pot for target practice, and the next burned down the tool shed and smeared filth on the parlor walls.

Now we're raiding, salvaging, harvesting, what you will. The house will be leaving us; we're taking out the things we want. It's half a shopping trip, half a wake. I can't decide whether it feels more callous to strip the house or to abandon family things to strangers. No matter how much furniture we carry out to the truck, the house seems to settle around what's left and make it look like enough, a trick learned in hard times, perhaps. It's difficult not to love a house that acts like that, but it's too late for love.

We didn't think there's be much we'd want, but objects that can be owned by us look all at once more desirable. We see how chairs would look with new upholstery. At the back of dark cupboards we find red glass plates, and a cup with "Brother" in gold script. Auntie Gyp's high-school class ring turns up in a painted box full of old postcards. We take down Grandmother's portrait and find the photo albums.

Murphy and I go a little wild. Our lives are still under-furnished; in fact, Murphy is still in college. I want the parlor stove. He wants to make the organ into a liquor cabinet. Our mother thinks we're crazy. I want the dining-room table. He wants to make the bookcase into a gun cabinet. She beats us away from faded quilts, hay rakes, the dining-room chairs. I can just remember this process at the dissolution of her childhood home, when I was six;

even then I wanted to take things, managed to drag home a pair of china figurines from a box full of desirable, abandoned stuff. She wouldn't even salvage Palilah, her earliest rag doll. "You don't want that. That's not worth anything," she kept, and keeps, saying.

I realize, though, that she still can't drive past her old house without pain, and I begin to understand, a little, what it's about. It seems necessary, though I'm close to thirty, to swing one more time from the lip of the stairwell, smelling the sour, dusty wood, to circle the buildings through the uncut grass, to stare once more into the ravine. For a few years after this I'll have strange dreams of a shining, beautified field somewhere through the woods behind the barn, and I'll wish then that I'd explored farther on this final day before we cut the farm loose to drift through memory and desire, this last day when it was nothing more than its solid, possibly underrated, self.

3

Murphy has most satisfactorily grown up, while my mother, who has always gone with the crowd, grows younger to meet us. We're learning to play together, to see how far we can go without getting killed. When I bitch one time too many about the heat, my mother slings a saucepan of cold water over me, right at the kitchen table, and says, "That better?" She spits down the back of Murphy's blue jeans when he bends over. What would my father have made of all this? He was playful and teasing, himself, liking for instance to come up behind us on a Bangor street and pretend to be a stranger bumping into us, but the games we play now are rowdier. We are feeling, for the first time, unsupervised. Not for us boiled shirts in the jungle. We're scrambling for our loin cloths.

We go down to the coast to see my mother's cousins for a summer day here and there. My father didn't hold much with cousins, his own or anyone else's, and these cousins, moreover, used to try kissing him Hello. He couldn't see any pleasure in visiting, ever, but my mother and Murphy and I quite like it.

Now that we see the cousins more often, we're finding our roles in the larger family drama. My mother is envied for her relationship with us, for having children who romp with her. Cousins who would never spit down their children's pants wonder what her secret is. Those cousins have built summer houses in a huge field on the coast, and we'll flit from house to house all day, sucking up the flavors of personality from the sisters who are my mother's contemporaries—the one who's sentimental and clever, the one who married big money and has lately taken to skinny dipping, the one who flings her legs over the arm of her chair and talks straight. Our great aunt, a vast and ancient woman with an unremitting Scots burr, will whop Murphy with her cane and cry, "Shave that beard! I canna stand the sight of it!" and he will be gratified.

4

Murphy, surprisingly, is getting married. We had him pegged for a lifelong bachelor but he was, it seems, just being frugal with his dating money. Now he's fetched a fiancée back from Winnipeg, where he's been doing graduate study, and my mother and I are giddy with the novelty. We haven't had a new family member since Murphy himself was born, and now here's this whole new relative, bringing along her own story like a character in a hypertext novel. We're delighted with Zirka from the start: she's bright and agreeable and funny, and comes with a bonus of cultural exoticism—she laughs at our struggles to say her name, while we find her lapses into Ukrainian consonant sounds no end endearing. Moreover she knows how to cook ethnic things we never heard of. She's at first a bit stunned by the skylarking of the family women, having come from a house where nobody whistles or fools around in front of the ikons, but she rallies—she's clearly made of flexible stuff. Only a few years from now she'll be wearing black leather skirts and driving a vicious bargain in Tibetan bazaars, and nobody will be surprised.

Her family are somewhat stunned as well. In Canada, American popularity is even lower than usual. Murphy not only isn't Ukrainian, he isn't even Catholic, though at least (as a kind aunt points out) the Baptists have a radio program. But the match is made and in Winnipeg they welcome us to the most exciting wedding we've ever seen, with gold crowns and book-kissing and exhortations in a tongue as mysteriously religious as glossolalia.

In the half day before our plane leaves, my mother and I go shopping at The Bay. By the time we're through at the regional gifts section we've lost our bearings completely, have no idea which way we came in. I stand vaguely waiting for my mother to lead, as she has, after all, done for my whole life. In a bit it occurs to me that nothing is happening. I look at her, and she's looking at me, clearly waiting for *me* to lead *her* out, this short, white-haired person that I'm suddenly supposed to be responsible for. I'm appalled. I can't believe that a major transition would happen this way, with no discussion. It's not as though one of us had just turned a milestone age. My mother has never announced, "I'm sixty-five now and retiring from management" or "You have now officially entered middle age and become the leader." She just gives me a trustful, dependent look. There's a moment when I can't catch my breath and I want to scream and protest that I'm not ready for this changing of the generations. But what's the use?

"I think it's over this way," I say, and she follows me.

*

Now we're selling Camp, that land of summer, and we've come to take away what we need to keep: doesn't this ever stop? It's the farm all over but worse: no avaricious discoveries here, only the dry cramp of hindsight—"we loved this." As we climb up the kitchen doorstep our hearts beat "last"—"last"—"last." Camp things loved for their very shabbiness seem too frail to take away. Even without my mother's restraining influence I probably wouldn't try to take away the ragged dish towels from the kitchen clothesline, the bent dipper from the water bucket. But I might. The feel of them goes deep.

Murphy wants, one more time, to walk up the shore to the point by wading through the edge of the lake, as he used to do in his teens. He invites me to go along. It's fun, a last lark, a boundary walk, a crazy tribute to wood and water. Up to our waists, sometimes our shoulders, in sharp, cool lake, we skid on slippery stones, grope our way around the wet side of boulders, peer past shoreline tree roots into the cedar darkness. We're rolling in the essence of place.

Before we leave we wipe off the oilcloth and sit down for a last supper, eating sandwiches off wax paper; we've packed the dishes. Once all these chairs were occupied and the camp was ours forever. I'm remembering a summer in the mid-Fifties when a tableful of family lingered after dinner every day to talk about dying. Or at any rate my father, Uncle Harris, and my maternal grandparents did. My mother and Osgood, the youngest adults, hated it. "They're at it again," they'd signal one another, and rush to clear and wash the dishes, anything to get away. Often as not I stayed from summer inertia, rubbing my finger over the oilcloth's pattern and watching Murphy play Davy Crockett between the trees while familiar sentences washed over me.

"By then I'll be pushing up the daisies," Uncle Harris always said.

"Well, the young *may* die but the old *must,*" someone else would remark. I didn't foresee then how these truths would unpeople my world.

Though my mother and Osgood, who fled to the kitchen, are still alive, in the end there's no place to run. One day not long enough from now my mother will have a stroke while reading the Secretary's report to a meeting of the Mission Circle, and never get to New Business. A surprise of the worst sort, but already Murphy and I understand, as we roll up our wax paper, what house we'll have to empty next.

ANN TRACY, born in rural Maine early in 1941, reports that like other War Babies she has never been quite able to shake the conviction that if you don't buy a thing when you see it, it'll be gone when you turn around. This is perhaps pertinent as well to memories and writing. She grew up in the pleasantly intense world of the rural coed boarding school of which her father was head and at which her mother sometimes taught Latin. A brother, later, grew to be an anthropologist and collector. Ann, who loved it all, after graduate school taught and wrote at SUNY Plattsburgh and decided in a late sabbatical to examine the effects and flavors of remembered whoop and lunacy.